THE HIDDEN KEY

To the O'Donnell Kids.

Enjoy!

Karen Tweedie

Written and Illustrated
by
Karen Simpson-Tweedie

To Mom and Dad, who gave me wings and taught me to fly strong and soar high. And to my husband, David, the love of my life.

Thanks to my brother, D.B.S., for his encouragement and immeasureably helpful advice; to S.B. for her wonderful suggestions while listening to the story as it developed; to M.W. and J.V. for keeping my historical facts straight, to G.H. at Miona Publications for loads of technical assistance and encouragement; to L.M. for much needed and appreciated graphic arts help; and to Nelly, sheep-dog extraordinaire, for being with me every day and every step of the way.

Published by Sheepdog Press,
PO Box 60, Onancock, VA 23417.

ISBN 0-9648393-6-9
A portion of the proceeds from the sale of each book will be donated to the Eastern Shore of Virginia Historical Society.

CONTENTS

Chapter 1
The Auction

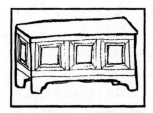 Like most girls her age, Megan was happy to be on vacation from school, but quite nervous about traveling so far to spend her vacation away from home. Besides, she wanted to be with her friends this summer. They had made plans to do all kinds of fun things, like play softball, and skate, and just hang around together. But Megan's grandparents had invited her to visit them at their summer home in Virginia and her parents decided she was old enough to go, alone! Her parents thought the timing of the invitation from Grandma and Grandpa was perfect, as Megan's father was going to be busy all summer after work in the evenings and on the weekends working on building an addition to their home. And Megan's mother, an author, was in the middle of a book and needed plenty of peace and quiet. In fact, Megan's dad was building an office for her mom. He hoped to have it completed by the middle of August, when Megan would return home, and they would all have a few weeks to spend together before school started again. Megan recalled her shock when her parents told her that she would be going to Virginia for the summer, by herself! Despite her protests and tears, her bags were packed and she boarded the airplane early this morning.

"We'll be landing in Norfolk in about forty-five minutes," announced the stewardess. "The temperature there is already 89 degrees. It's going to be a hot one."

Megan shifted in her seat and tried to look out the window. She wondered what Virginia looked like. This was her first trip to her grandparents' summer home. Megan's parents had told her many stories of their adventures growing up, when both had spent summers with their families on the Eastern Shore. That was where they had met, in fact, at a summer camp, more than twenty years ago. Megan hoped that her summer would be as much fun as her mother said it would be, but she was feeling rather jittery about the whole plan. She loved her grandparents, and had just seen them when they came for a visit during the Christmas holidays. But this was different. She had never been away from home for more than an overnight at a friend's house, and couldn't imagine being away for so long, for two whole months! She knew she would be homesick and miss her parents, but because they were always busy working, she imagined they would hardly notice that she wasn't there.

The plane landed smoothly and Megan quickly checked around her seat to make sure she hadn't forgotten anything. Her mother had reminded her over and over that she would have to take care of herself this summer, and she wanted this vacation to start out on the right foot. She anxiously followed the other passengers down the long walkway and out into the terminal.

"Megan, honey, over here!" she heard her grandfather call out.

Megan was relieved to hear her name and burst into a grin as she rushed over to her grandparents' outstretched arms.

"How was your flight?" asked her grandmother.

"Oh, it was fine."

"Are you hungry, Megan? I thought we could grab a bite here at the airport while we wait," said Grandpa.

"Wait? What are we waiting for?" she asked.

"You mean your parents didn't tell you? Well, that's just like your mother. Always the mystery writer, that girl. We're waiting for your cousin, Kendall, to arrive. Her flight is due to arrive in just about an hour. That gives us enough time to eat something and start catching up. What have you been up to? How was school?"

Megan chatted with her grandparents over lunch, and silently wondered about her cousin, Kendall. She and Kendall were about the same age, but they hadn't seen each other for many years. In fact, Megan really didn't know Kendall at all. They had been together a few times during family vacations when the girls were very young, but Megan had been too little to remember. Kendall lived in New Hampshire, very far away from Megan's home in California. Megan's mother and Kendall's mother were sisters, and they kept in close contact. So Megan heard stories all the time about the wonderful things Kendall was doing. Unlike Megan, Kendall was a star student and seemed to do everything well. She hoped that Kendall's visit would be a short one. Megan was an only child and was used to being the only child around. Since she felt she hadn't seen much of her parents lately, she planned to spend plenty of time with her grandparents this summer, alone.

Kendall closed her book and tucked it into her backpack. She glanced at her watch and saw that the flight was on time. She would be landing in a few minutes. Kendall was excited to see Grandma and Grandpa. Things had been difficult at home this past year, and Kendall needed this time away. At home she had too many responsibilities. She felt she spent all her time looking after her two younger brothers and helping around the house with cleaning and lately even with some of the cooking. Her mother was always telling her how much she needed Kendall and depended on her. She looked forward to being the only child for a change. Her two brothers were spending the summer at camp, and Kendall couldn't wait to spend long, lazy days with Grandma and Grandpa at their summer home. It would be fun to be an only child for a change.

"Kendall, honey, we're over here!" she heard Grandpa call. Kendall waved in reply as she made her way past all of the passengers with their bags and suit-cases. She broke into a wide smile as she approached her grandparents.

"Hi, Grandma! Hi, Grandpa! Oh, I'm so happy to see you."

"You look wonderful, Kendall. I'm so glad you can be with us for the summer," said Grandma. "And did you know that Megan is going to be with us, too? Isn't that wonderful?"

In all the confusion of the other passengers, Kendall hadn't noticed the shy young girl standing next to her grandparents.

"Megan?" Kendall stared at the small girl. " I didn't know you were coming." She turned quickly to face her grandmother. "Grandma, why didn't you tell me about Megan?" she asked irritably.

"I guess it slipped my mind," said her grandmother
with a smile, "but both of your mothers knew. Those
girls of mine are something else! I guess they wanted
you two to be surprised. Well, let's go gather up your
things, Kendall, and then we can head back across the
bay to the Shore. I'm sure you're both tired, and I want
to get you two settled in."

Megan silently watched out the car window as they
drove north to her grandparents' summer home. She
marveled at the long bridge they crossed and the rugged
stretch of land on the other side. Grandpa explained that
settlers had lived on the Eastern Shore since the early
1600s, and before that, the only inhabitants were the
Algonquian Indians. Early settlers from Jamestown
came to the Shore because of the plentiful fish and salt.
Many of the names of towns and creeks are Indian
names, Grandpa said.

She listened as Kendall and Grandma laughed and
talked about all sorts of things. Megan realized that
Kendall was as close to Grandma as she was, and she felt
a twinge of jealousy. This turn of events, with Kendall
showing up, had Megan feeling even more upset than
she had been during her whole long flight. She was
afraid that her grandparents would spend their time
with Kendall, and Megan would once again be left alone.
Kendall seemed to know what to talk about. After all,
Megan's mother was always talking about how terrific
Kendall was. Now Megan would have to spend the
summer in the shadow of Kendall. This is just great, she
thought with a sigh. She was starting to realize that she
spent an awful lot of time feeling lonely. And she was
dreading two lonely months in a strange place.

Kendall listened as Grandma talked excitedly about

activities she had been planning for the girls. Grandma
loved all kinds of arts and crafts. She had been a teacher
for years and was now retired. Kendall glanced at
Megan who was staring out the window. Kendall
couldn't believe that her cousin was here. She had been
looking forward to spending time with Grandma and
Grandpa without the responsibilities of home. Kendall
knew she and Megan were about the same age, but
thought Megan looked younger and hoped that she
wouldn't have to baby-sit her for the summer. That
would be all she needed!

The next few days passed quickly. The girls were
busy helping Grandma and Grandpa open up the house
for the summer. That meant there was a lot of work to be
done! Everything had to be swept and washed and
carried upstairs and down. Megan loved the big, old
house. It was so different from her home in California.
She loved her little bedroom at the top of the stairs.
Kendall's room was just down the hall.

On the third morning, Grandpa got up early and
went to an auction. Grandma had errands to run, so the
girls were left to themselves for the first time. Working
alongside the grandparents they both adored, the girls
had developed a tentative friendship, and a truce. Neither had known that the other was coming, and they had
both felt a little jealous about sharing the attention of
their grandparents, but it was actually working out fine.
Megan wasn't nearly as homesick as she thought she
might be, and Kendall was more relaxed than she had
been in a long time.

The girls spent the morning sitting on the front porch
talking about their grandparents and playing cat's
cradle. Megan thought Kendall was funny and was

relieved Kendall didn't talk about school. Kendall thought Megan was shy, but found her to be interesting and fun to talk with. Just as they were getting up to take a walk to explore the neighborhood, Grandpa pulled up in his old pickup truck.

"Got you girls something at the auction. Come on down and help me get it out of the truck," Grandpa called out.

The girls watched as Grandpa lowered the back of the truck. "What is it?" asked Megan curiously as she looked at the big blue and white painted box.

"It's a blanket chest, a real old one. You girls can use it to store your treasures in this summer. I thought we could put it upstairs in the hallway. I think it needs to be cleaned up a bit first, though."

"Oh, great, more cleaning," groaned Kendall.

The girls helped guide the heavy box up onto the porch. It was big and covered with years of dust and grime.

"Ever been to an auction?" asked Grandpa.

"No, not me," answered Kendall.

"Me neither," said Megan.

"Want to come back to the auction with me, then? There are some real interesting things this time. Lots of stuff from a very old house in town. You might find something you like. Here's some pocket money for you two to share. You earned it with all of your hard work these past few days."

"Thanks, Grandpa," said Kendall as she stuffed the bills deep into her pocket. "But I don't know how an auction works. I don't know what to do."

"It's easy. Jump into the truck and I'll give you a quick lesson in auction buying while we drive over there."

"Let's go," Megan laughed as she raced Kendall to the truck.

The air was warm as the girls walked slowly up and down the rows of boxes and piles of things for sale at the auction, some familiar, some strange. Grandpa had explained how to buy at the auction, had gotten them a bidding number, and sent them on their own. He was standing to the side with a group of men looking over some old farm equipment. In the background was the constant drone of the auctioneer. "Who will give me two, two, two dollars, now three, three, now four, five, six, six, six, anyone for six, six, going, going, sold for five dollars to number 46. Next item now, here's a good one! Who will start me out at five, five, five..."

In the last row Kendall spotted a tall cardboard box with brightly colored yarn on the top. "Hey, Megan, look at this stuff."

Megan touched the yarn, then lifted up a handful. "It's really pretty. Maybe Grandma would like this. She could make something with it, or maybe even teach us how to knit. What else is in the box?"

"I don't know, there's lots of other stuff under the yarn. Some material, and other stuff at the bottom." Kendall was bent down trying to look further into the big box when she suddenly stopped digging and stood up. "Megan," she whispered sharply. "This stuff looks really old! There's some kind of old box, maybe a jewelry box, and lots of other stuff. I think we should buy this box."

"Can I see?" exclaimed Megan excitedly as she started pulling yarn from the top of the box.

"Wait!" Kendall whispered. "Remember what

Grandpa told us. He said sometimes you find really neat stuff hiding in boxes but the trick is to not draw a lot of attention to it. That way there aren't tons of other people looking, too."

"Oh. Well, what should we do?"

"Let's keep moving down the row to the end and pretend to look at the rest of the stuff, but keep an eye on our box."

The auctioneer finished selling some old chairs then moved over to the last row. "Folks, as soon as I finish up with these boxes here, I'll be selling the beautiful set of Victorian parlor furniture over there under the tree. If you haven't looked it over, better do it now. It's real pretty. Haven't seen anything this nice in a long time." The crowd of people drifted over toward the tree, leaving just a few standing with the auctioneer. "Let's finish up with these boxes. Now who will give me five for this one? Real nice kitchen stuff here. Five? Four? How about three, three, three dollars, got three, now four, four, four? Sold for three dollars to you, sir."

The girls stood nervously at the edge of the group of bidders. Their box was coming up next.

"Here's a fine bunch of yarn for you ladies out there. And lots of other stuff, too. Big box, you never know what you might find. Who will start me out with twenty dollars?"

"Twenty dollars?" whispered Kendall to Megan with growing concern. "I thought he would start it at two dollars like the other ones. We don't have that much money. But we have to get that box!" The girls didn't know what to do.

"Twenty, twenty, anyone bidding twenty? Ten, ten, anyone gonna give me ten? Come on, folks, let's get this started. How 'bout five, five, five?" The crowd under the tree was growing and forming a deepening circle around a big desk. A man was pulling out the drawers and examining them carefully. It caught the attention of the bidders standing with the auctioneer and they walked over to join the crowd. "Who will give me three, three, three dollars for this nice box? Okay, start me at two, two, two dollars, anyone, two?" the auctioneer pleaded.

Megan elbowed Kendall and Kendall raised up their bidding card so that the auctioneer could see her.

"Two now, I have two, anyone three, three, three? This is a nice big box here. You're missing out on some real treasures. Come on back over here, folks. Two, two, I've got two, now who will give me three dollars? Three?" The auctioneer sighed, "Sold for two dollars to you two girls. Got yourselves a great bargain there, ladies."

"We got it! I can't believe it! Let's go tell Grandpa," shouted Kendall with glee.

CHAPTER 2
TREASURES

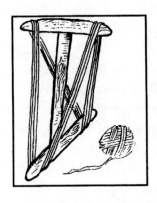

M egan, look at this stuff! There are all kinds of things in here. And here is a big bundle of old material all tied up. Maybe it's somebody's old fabric collection? Grandma would love that. Here, I'm going to hand the bundle to you and you can set it down on the porch swing, okay?" Kendall was bent over and half buried in the big box. "Oh, this is strange. I think there's something wrapped up inside this fabric. It must be pretty old, so we need to be careful."

Megan was carefully arranging the balls of colorful yarn beside the tall cardboard box as Kendall stood back up holding a large roll of blue and white material in both hands.

"My, you girls certainly look busy," exclaimed Grandma. "What's all this?"

"We bought this whole box of pretty yarn at the auction with Grandpa and there's more stuff buried underneath it," said Megan cheerfully.

"Goodness, Kendall, that fabric is wonderful. It looks like some nice old homespun. I remember having that around when I was a girl," said Grandma as she touched the bundle of blue and white fabric that Kendall was holding.

"Well, I think there's something wrapped up inside of it," exclaimed Kendall as she gently handed it to Megan.

The three huddled close together as Megan carefully untied the strip of fabric that was wound around the material and started to slowly unwrap the bundle.

"Oh, my gosh. Look at this pretty little doll. And here's an old spoon. And look at that little bottle. I can't believe it!" said Megan. She gently picked up the rag doll and cradled it in her arms.

"You girls have really found something here," said Grandma. "That's a very old rag doll, Megan, and some-one took great care of her, because she's hardly worn at all. This bottle is interesting. I think it's an old ink bottle. See the dried ink in the bottom? And this spoon, hmm, do you want me to take it inside and polish it up for you? It might look better cleaned up a bit."

"Oh, Grandma, thanks. This is so exciting! And there's more stuff in the box," said Kendall as she dove back down into the tall box.

"What else is in there, Kendall?" said Megan with growing excitement as she carefully set the doll on the porch swing. "Let's get the rest of the stuff out of the box so we can see what we have!"

When Grandpa stepped out onto the porch a short time later, the girls' treasures were all arranged on the porch swing.

"Looks like you girls hit the jackpot," said Grandpa. "Did all of that come out of the box you bought at the auction?"

"Yeah, look at this stuff, Grandpa! What do you think?"

"Well, when I was talking with the auctioneer, he hadn't realized who you girls were when he saw you

bidding at the auction. When he found out you two are
my granddaughters, he told me something that I think
you'll find pretty interesting. He said that yesterday,
when they were getting ready for the auction, they
opened up the blanket chest and it was full of stuff. So
they got a big, tall box and dumped everything out of the
blanket chest and into the box. And that happens to be
the box you two bought. Imagine that? All of this was in
the blanket chest yesterday. Lucky thing no one else
bought it, huh?"

"I can't believe it," said Kendall. "All this was inside
of that dirty old blanket chest? Well, we can clean it up
and then we can store our treasures right back in the
chest, okay, Megan?"

"Sure, that's the perfect place for it. I wonder who
owned the blanket chest? Do you know who put it in the
auction, Grandpa?"

"I don't, but I can try to find out. I'll talk to the auctioneer later on and see what I can find out." Grandpa
spotted a small wooden box on the swing. "That's a real
nice little box there. May I see it?"

"Here, Grandpa. But I can't get it opened," said
Megan as she handed her grandfather the box.

"This is a keyhole here in the front. Hmmm, it looks
like it's locked. You didn't find a key in there anyplace,
did you?" Grandpa asked as he set the box down.

"No, there's no key," said Megan disappointedly as
she picked up the rag doll. "But just look at this other
stuff. I don't even know what it all is, but it's neat!"

"Hmm, old clay marbles. These are great. And that
little wooden cradle is nice. You can put your doll right
in. Someone took some time making this cradle," said
Grandpa as he turned it over and examined it. "And
look at this wooden plate. It could be an Indian plate.

This is very interesting. And quite old, I'm sure. Do you know what these are, girls?" asked Grandpa as he picked up a strange scissor-like tool.

"No, Grandpa. What is it?" asked Megan.

"I'm not positive, but I think these are sugar cutters. I've never seen real ones, just in pictures. A long time ago, sugar came in a big cone shaped piece, called a loaf. In order to use the sugar, you had to cut off some of the loaf. That's when they used these sugar cutters, to cut off lumps of sugar. Sugar was very expensive back then, and people were very careful with it. These sugar cutters would have been an important kitchen tool. I'd like to borrow these, if you girls don't mind, and show them to the fellow at the local museum to make sure I'm right about them."

Grandma opened the front door and walked back onto the large porch. "How do you like your spoon now, girls?" She handed the shiny silver spoon to Megan.

"Wow, this is beautiful. Thanks, Grandma!"

"I noticed that there are three initials on the end. They're a bit difficult to make out, but I think it says A.J.M.," said Grandma.

"That was in the box, too?" asked Grandpa. "What else did you find?"

"There's this funny twisted wooden thing, and a little sewing piece. I think you saw everything else. Oh, except for the letters. We haven't opened them yet," said Kendall as she stood next to the collection of objects piled high on the swing.

"Yeah, I put them over there," said Megan. "I'm almost afraid to touch them, they look so old. I want to wash my hands first so I don't get them dirty." She pointed to a small stack of carefully folded letters, plainly and neatly addressed, and tied with a narrow width of fabric.

"Those look wonderful," said Grandma. "We can read them later, inside. I think I know what the wooden thing is. It looks like a niddy noddy."

"A what?" laughed Megan.

"A niddy noddy. They were used to wind homespun yarn on, to make it straight and keep it from getting all tangled up. You might want to wind some of your pretty yarn on it, Megan."

"Great idea. And what about this sewing piece?"

Grandma picked up the small piece of tan fabric and looked it over carefully. "Girls, this may be the best treasure yet. This is an old sampler, something that young girls stitched when they were learning to embroider. 'Steadfast and True. Anah Jane Matthews. July 6, 1808.' And here is the alphabet, and flowers and birds. This is just beautiful. The colors are still bright. The stitches look like they're done in silk and wool. It was done on a piece of woven canvas. Well, we know how old this piece is."

"You mean it was made in 1808?" asked Kendall incredulously.

"Sure looks like it," said Grandpa. "I think you girls should come to the museum with me and bring all of this. The man there might be able to give you some more information. I've never seen so many wonderful pieces all together. And I'd like to know who they belonged to, and how they ended up in that old blanket chest. He might be able to help us solve this mystery."

"Mystery?" whispered Megan to herself.

CHAPTER 3
LETTERS

After dinner, Grandma and the girls sat down together and untied the bundle of letters. Grandma carefully unfolded the first letter and began to read the writing on the yellowed paper.

September 15, 1809

My dear cousin Anah,

I love the cool, crisp air in the mornings this time of year. The weather is cool and the trees are full of apples. Soon we will pick them and I will string lots of apples to dry for the winter. It is hard work, but we will be glad to have them when the snow is on the ground!

Today I visited Grandmother and Grandfather Watson and they are both well. Grandmother is busy stitching a lovely quilt for our newest cousin, Uncle Hutchinson's and Aunt Mary's daughter, Dorothy Watson. Dorothy is a beautiful, healthy baby. I saw her yesterday. It was fun playing with her. She laughs and smiles a lot.

My brother, Daniel improves his whittling each day. He works so seriously with his penknife. He made a likeness of a bird that is quite lovely. He also made a whistle for little Dorothy, but she is too young to use it yet. I taught Daniel to play your cat's cradle game that you taught me last summer!

My chores are finished for today. I have milked the cows, helped Mother with mending, ironing, and spooling. We are combing and carding wool from our sheep for spinning this winter.

I am anxious to visit with you again in the spring, dear cousin. It will be wonderful to see you, Uncle Edwin, Aunt Elizabeth and your brothers. Write to me when you are able.

Your cousin,

Eliza Edmonds

Grandma unfolded the second letter and read from the ancient handwriting as the girls listened attentively!

February 3, 1810

My dear cousin Anah,

The snow is falling still. Mother and I have been busy spinning wool from our sheep. By the end of this winter we should have enough wool to begin weaving a blanket. Daniel and I try to stay in the kitchen to keep warm. It is our job to keep wood piled on the firedogs all day. The water in the bowl in my bedroom was frozen this morning because it was so cold, and ink freezes in our quills if we move them out of the kitchen. At night I bury myself in my feather bed and pull the curtains closed tight. Otherwise, I feel I would surely freeze in my sleep!

Tonight Daniel is playing with his marbles

and I am sewing. I am sewing a baby with scraps from Mother's old dress. The baby is beautiful and I named her Nelly.

I hope you and your family are healthy. Grandmother and Grandfather Watson are doing well. I visited with them yesterday. Uncle Richard is staying with them for the winter to help with the chores.

I look forward to spring.

Your cousin,

Eliza Edmonds

Megan was holding the rag doll in her arms while Grandma read the letters. "Do you think this is Nelly?" she asked with surprise as she looked at the old hand-made doll.

"Well, I guess that's possible, but there's no way to really know that, Megan. But someone made that doll with loving hands."

Kendall placed the second letter on the stack with the others. "Thanks for helping us read these letters, Grandma. I wish I knew who these people were," she said. "Reading these letters is like getting a little peek into their lives, but I want to know more about them. I wonder about their families and school, and stuff like that."

"Life back then was quite different than it is today," said Grandma. "Settlers worked very hard just to keep a roof over their heads and food on the table. And clothes on their backs. They had to know how to make or grow nearly everything they needed. And they didn't have so many things that we have and use everyday without even thinking about it. Like electricity. Think about how many things in our house here run off of electricity. Without electricity, simple jobs become much more difficult and take a very long time. Like doing the laundry, for example. We can just gather up the dirty clothes and pop them into the washer, add some soap from the store, push a button, and we're done. Can you imagine if each piece of clothing had to be washed and rinsed by hand? And they didn't have running water then either. All the water had to be brought up from a well or in from a stream and heated on a wood fire if you wanted it warm. And the soap? They had to make that, too. Making soap was a job that lasted all day. And children had to share in the responsibilities of the household. Everyone worked very hard, but they had fun back then, too."

"Who are all of those people in the letters?" asked Megan.

"Well, it seems like one cousin is writing to another cousin about their families. These letters are very old, from 1809 and 1810. One cousin is named Eliza Edmonds and her cousin is Anah Matthews. See here on the outside of the letter is her name, just like we write on an envelope. And she lived in Accomac, right here in this town. It's amazing that these letters have lasted all this time. And isn't the handwriting lovely? It was very important back then for children to learn to have beautiful writing. They practiced it a lot. Notice how the letters look different from the way you girls write now? That's why it's a little bit difficult for you to read her writing. Well, it's been a long day, and now it's time for bed. We can read the rest of the letters in the morning. You girls get a good night's sleep. This has been quite an exciting day."

"Love you, Grandma," said both girls as they kissed her good night.

A short time later Megan was sitting on her bed in her cozy little room holding the rag doll. She wondered again if this was the doll from the letters. It was a very exciting thought. She jumped when she heard a sharp knock at the door and before she could get up to open it, Kendall walked in and sat down beside her on the bed.

"You really like that doll, don't you?" Kendall observed. "Can you believe that we get to be here for two whole months? Isn't this fun?"

Megan just nodded.

"I've been packed for weeks! I couldn't wait to leave home and come here." Kendall paused. "You're so lucky."

"Me? Why am I so lucky?" asked Megan with surprise.

"Because it's just you and your parents." Kendall hesitated before going on. "I have two younger brothers and I feel like their mother. I make their lunches in the morning before school and have to watch them everyday after school. All they do is fight and they're so noisy. And now my mom is teaching me to cook so that I can make dinner on the nights that she gets home late," revealed Kendall slowly.

"Really? But what about your dad?" asked Megan

with concern.

"He's not home much. He has a new job that's pretty far away so he stays there during the week and just comes home on weekends. And not every weekend." She paused. "I think he and Mom are having problems, but they don't talk about it."

"Kendall, that's, um, I'm so sorry."

"Yeah, it's been pretty rough this past year, so that's why I was so excited when Mom said Grandma and Grandpa had invited me for the summer. I thought I would be the only kid here, but this is nice having you here, too. What about you? Weren't you excited when you found out you could come here for the whole summer?"

"Well, actually, no. I wanted to be home and do stuff with my friends and do stuff with Mom and Dad."

"But you're with them all the time. Doesn't your mom work at home? That's what my mom told me."

"Oh, she's home, but she's always working, writing books, so she can't be disturbed. When she's in the middle of a book, Dad cooks dinner or he and I go out and get something."

"That must be nice to spend so much time with your dad. I haven't had dinner with just my dad since, well, never."

"Yeah, Dad's great. But he has work to do at night, too, so I'm mostly by myself at home. And I have to spend a lot of time doing homework." Megan looked down at the doll in her arms. "Everyone knows my mom is a writer, so they expect me to do something special all the time, and I don't. I try, but my school work is just okay. Nothing great. I thought that this summer we would have time to do stuff together as a

family, because Mom said she's almost done with her
book and Dad didn't have as much work to bring home.
But then they both got busy and Mom thought I should
come here," finished Megan quietly.

"Oh, that's too bad. Well, we don't have to think
about that stuff right now, okay? So, what do you like to
do?"

Megan thought for a moment before answering.
"Well, I like to do puzzles, you know, like jigsaw
puzzles, and games where you have to figure stuff out.
My mom and I used to always do puzzles together.
Once, when she was stuck on a part in one of her books,
she talked about it with me and I helped her figure out
how to solve the problem! That was so much fun."
Megan laughed just thinking about it. "What about you?
What do you like to do?"

"Well, I don't have much time to do anything fun, but
I like to do sports, and I like to do art stuff, like Grandma
does."

"Me, too. I like to make things. I'm hoping that
Grandma will teach us how to make some neat things."

"Yeah, that would be great. She's so much fun. And
so is Grandpa. I'm really glad I get to be here this summer," said Kendall.

"Yeah, me too," agreed Megan. "I think this is going
to be a fun summer after all!"

CHAPTER 4
THE KEY

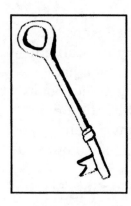

Can you girls give me a hand moving this blanket chest upstairs? It's a little awkward and I need some help guiding it up the stairs."

"Sure, Grandpa. We got the dust cleaned off and wiped down the inside yesterday," replied Kendall.

The three of them lifted the heavy painted chest up and carried it through the front door and into the hallway to the bottom of the stairs. "We can just tilt it up a little and get it up the stairs. Kendall, you get in the front and help guide it. Megan, your job is to make sure we don't bump the wall."

Grandpa tilted the chest up and they heard a funny sliding noise, then a small thump!

"What was that?" asked Megan.

"Guess there was something left inside," said Grandpa.

"No, it was completely empty. We just wiped it down with a cloth and there wasn't anything inside," said Kendall.

"Well, we will open her up when we get upstairs and take a look. Are we going straight?"

"Yeah, just a few more steps to go, Grandpa."

They set the blanket chest down in the hall outside Megan's bedroom. "Darn, we have it turned the wrong way so that the open side is to the wall. Let's turn it around. I'll just pick up this end and we can pivot it around the other way," said Grandpa.

He picked up the end and they heard the funny sliding noise, then a thump again!

"There it is again. I don't know what we missed when we cleaned it out!" exclaimed Kendall.

"Let's see." Grandpa opened the large blanket chest and the three peered inside.

"It's empty," said Megan.

"Then what was that noise?" asked Kendall.

"Hmmm, it's a mystery to me," said Grandpa. "Maybe there's a loose hinge or something. Are you girls ready to go to Kerr Place with me? That's our local museum over in the next town, Onancock. It used to be the home of the Kerr family. The curator is anxious to see what you two have discovered."

"Car Place? That's a funny name," said Kendall. "It sounds like a place you go to buy a car."

"Kerr was the last name of the family that built the house, but it is spelled differently than the word for automobile. It's K-e-r-r."

"Oh, that's neat."

"I'm ready," said Megan.

"Me, too," said Kendall as the two girls raced down the stairs.

"This is an extremely interesting collection you girls have discovered," said the man as he lifted their treasures out of the large cardboard box one at a time. "Very unusual to find objects in such good condition that are this old. Now where did you say you found these things? At an auction?"

"Yeah, we went with Grandpa to an auction and we bought a big box of yarn and there was all this stuff down underneath. Some of it was wrapped up in old material that Grandma called homespun," explained Kendall.

"Be careful with that homespun fabric. Homespun means that the cotton or wool was spun on a spinning wheel by hand, and then someone wove the fabric on a loom. It took hours to card the material for spinning, which is like brushing it out straight. Then hours more to spin enough yarn for weaving. It took hundreds of hours to card, spin, and weave a small blanket or material for clothes. There isn't a lot of homespun left anymore because it was used for clothing and bedding and just wore out. Your doll here is made of homespun and I imagine at one time the little girl who owned her had a homespun blanket that fit into this cradle. Hmmm, this box is lovely. It's a shame it's locked."

"We didn't find the key," said Kendall.

"Well, I don't want to force it open because that could break it. If you don't mind, I'd like to keep it here for a few days. I have a cabinetry expert coming in at the end of the week and I would like him to take a look at these wooden pieces. I would like to examine this wooden plate. It is a very typical example of household items from the early 1800s. Do you girls know what this is?" the curator asked as he picked up a wooden piece with two perpendicular end pieces, each at right angles to the other.

"Grandma said it is a niddy noddy," said Megan.

"That's right. The family who owned this probably raised sheep and had a spinning wheel and a loom, too. And this sampler is extraordinary. 'Steadfast and True. Anah Jane Matthews. July 6, 1808.' Fabulous example of an early sampler. Marvelous conditon. The colors in the stitching are still bright. Amazing. Let's see what else is here. You have a nice start on an old clay marble collection. This big one here would have been the shooter. I started collecting glass marbles when I was a young boy. My prize marble is a taw, which is a large, fancy marble. Then I have my favorite alley, which was my shooter, some agates, some bloodstone, and several steelies. I think I even have a few tiger eyes. You know, I haven't looked at that collection in a long time. And your grandfather was right about these sugar cutters. They are quite rare. I haven't seen one in person before, only photos in several books. Nice little ink bottle here, and this spoon is certainly silver, a very early piece. Hmm, A.J.M. This may have belonged to the girl who made the sampler, Anah Jane Matthews. This is quite a lovely spoon. Very old and appears to be from Scotland. You can tell that from these markings here on the back. They're called hallmarks and they indicate where and when a silver piece was made, as well as who the maker was. There were some Scots who settled in this area about two hundred years ago. One wealthy Scotsman, John Shepherd Kerr, began building the house we are in right now in 1799. So it makes sense to find this Scottish piece here. You girls have a wonderful collection of historical artifacts. They tell a story about the lives of people who lived a long time ago. Is this everything you found?"

"Well, there are some letters, too, but we left them at

home," answered Kendall.

The curator was interested. "I would very much like to see them sometime. You'll have to take special care with all these things to make sure they don't get damaged. It's best to keep them away from the light as much as possible."

"They're going to keep everything inside a blanket chest we have upstairs," said Grandpa.

"That's a good idea," said the curator as he carefully placed all but the wooden objects back in the box. "Blanket chests are wonderful for storage. Very practical pieces of furniture. People have been using them for hundreds of years. We have several here in the museum. Families kept most anything in them and used them when they moved. They were passed down from generation to generation in some families. Sometimes they have built in drawers or smaller boxes inside. And a few have even been known to have a false bottom for hiding valuables. "

The girls looked at each other with wide eyes while Grandpa listened to the curator. "False bottom!" mouthed Megan to Kendall and Kendall nodded in acknowledgment.

"We find examples of the old painted raised-panel chests from time to time here on the Shore. They're usually made of yellow pine and are painted blue and white. They're quite rare and are highly sought after," the curator explained.

"We may have ourselves a real antique, girls. The old blanket chest I bought at the auction might be one of the raised-panel ones the curator was talking about," said

Grandpa as they drove back home. "I asked him to stop by sometime and take a look."

The girls looked at each other in silence. Finally Megan spoke nervously, "Grandpa, remember the funny noises we heard when we moved the blanket chest? Do you think our chest has a false bottom like the curator was talking about? Maybe there's something hidden inside and that's what we heard."

"Hold on, girls. We can't start tearing apart a fine old piece of furniture like that just to look for a loose nail or something. That's probably all it was. Now, let's not go overboard with this treasure hunt stuff. You hit the jackpot with that big box you bought at the auction. Have you finished reading all of the letters yet?"

"No, not yet. They're pretty hard to read because the writing is so different. Grandma is helping us with the letters," answered Kendall.

They drove the rest of the way home in silence.

A light flashed around the room and Megan awoke with a start. "What are you doing?" she asked her cousin. Balls of colorful yarn were piled on the floor. Kendall was setting objects on the floor with one hand and held a flashlight in the other.

"Shh, we don't want to wake up Grandma and Grandpa," whispered Kendall.

"But what are you doing?" Megan asked again.

"You and I are going to take a closer look at that blanket chest and see for ourselves if there is a false bottom."

"But Grandpa said we can't tear the chest apart! We'll get in trouble," cried Megan.

"Don't worry, we aren't going to mess it up. I just

want to look the chest over and see if we can find anything. Are you going to help me?"

"Okay, but I hope we don't wake up Grandma and Grandpa," Megan agreed nervously.

"Don't worry. Just tiptoe out into the hall with me and let's see if we can see anything inside the chest. I took everything out and put it here in your room. The chest is empty again."

The girls moved silently into the hall. The lid to the chest was already open as Kendall shined the light inside. "I don't see anything," whispered Megan. "It just looks like an empty box to me."

"I know, but I also know we heard something moving around in here. I have no idea what a false bottom looks like. We can't flip this thing over. It's too heavy and it would definitely wake up Grandma and Grandpa."

"And then we would definitely get in trouble," added Megan.

"Just relax. You hold the light up here while I reach around inside and see if I feel anything. Maybe there's a little loose nail that is stuck around an edge or something. That could have made the noise."

Kendall reached deep into the chest and felt around all four sides. "No, I don't feel anything stuck down the edges."

"Can I try?" asked Megan.

"Sure, I'll hold the light for you. See if you feel anything, I don't know, anything that feels funny. I wish I knew what we were looking for."

Megan leaned all the way over and reached deep into the chest. She felt the smooth sides of the chest, then ran her hands across the bottom. Suddenly she stopped. "That's funny," she said.

"What did you find?" asked Kendall excitedly.

"I didn't find anything, but there is a funny little dip in the wood here on the bottom. Maybe the person who made the chest made a little mistake here, 'cause the wood isn't even like the rest of it. The whole rest of the inside is even and smooth, but there's a little dip, like about the size of a little marble. I can put my thumb right into the dip!"

"Can I see?" asked Kendall. She moved the flashlight over to the place where Megan was holding her thumb, but accidently bumped Megan's arm.

"Oh! I think I broke something," Megan whispered.

"What do you mean?" asked Kendall worriedly.

"When you bumped my arm, my thumb pushed down and the board popped up a little bit. I think I broke something. Oh, Kendall, now what do we do?"

"The wood popped up? Where? Show me where!" said Kendall with growing excitement.

"Right here," whispered Megan.

Kendall placed her hand on the spot that Megan showed her and felt around the edges of the loosened board. She was able to get her fingers on either side of the board and held on tight, then pulled up slowly. To her surprise, the board pulled up easily and popped right out.

"Megan, you found it! You found the false bottom!" She shined the light into the opening made by the missing board. "I don't see anything down in there, though."

"Want me to put my hand in and see if I can find anything?" Megan leaned over and reached her hand down into the opening. She felt around the sides of a small box hidden under the floor of the chest. Her fingers ran around the edges of the box. Nothing. Then she flattened her hand and ran it over the bottom of the hidden box. She gasped.

"What?" Kendall whispered.

"I found it! I found it!" Megan replied breathlessly.

Kendall's light followed Megan's closed hand as she pulled it up and out of the chest. Megan opened her balled fist and there it was in her palm, a key.

CHAPTER 5

CANDLES

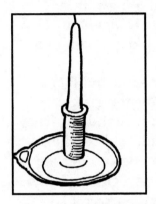

Megan woke just as the sun came up. She had barely slept at all, what with the excitement of finding the key in the trunk last night! Kendall had replaced the false bottom and the girls had carefully placed everything back into the trunk before they tiptoed off to bed. Kendall said that since Megan found the key, Megan should be the person to keep it safe. Megan had set the key on the table right next to her bed and woke up several times during the night to check on it. In the light of the morning, she picked it up and studied it carefully. It was long and narrow with a circle on one end and a notched piece on the other. It looked quite old, but she couldn't be sure. But Megan was sure of one thing. This was the key to the little locked wooden box. She just knew it.

At breakfast the girls were jittery with excitement about their discovery of the key, but they didn't want to tell their grandparents, at least not yet. It was fun to have a secret to share. All they wanted to do was get back to the museum to get their box and try out the key.

"Grandpa, can you take us back to the museum

today?" asked Kendall.

"Girls, you need to get outside and have some fun.
Let's go out on the boat and head out to the barrier
islands. We can do some fishing and look for shells. It'll
be great. Megan, have you ever been fishing before?"

"No, but I guess it sounds like fun," she said reluc-
tantly.

"Come on girls. Put on your swimming suits and
let's get going. It's too warm to hang around here. Let's
get out on the water. You can swim all day if you like,"
Grandpa finished excitedly.

Their day was filled with sun and sand and lots of
fun. Grandpa caught several fish while the girls ex-
plored the beach of the tiny island with Grandma. They
swam in the protected water on the inlet side of the
island, then crossed over to the other side and danced in
the waves of the Atlantic Ocean. It was a glorious day
and the girls completely forgot about their secret key.

That evening after dinner as the girls were clearing
the table Grandma said, "Would you girls like to use
some of that pretty yarn you have? I thought it would be
fun to teach you how to make a little yarn doll. I remember making one when I was about your age.

"That's sounds fun. How do we make one?" asked
Megan.

"It's pretty easy. Run upstairs and get some yarn and
I'll show you how. All we need is a pair of scissors, yarn,
and a piece of cardboard."

Grandma showed the girls how to wind yarn around
the cardboard long ways several times, tie it with a
shorter piece of yarn, then cut it off the cardboard. Then
they wound up small balls of yarn to form the head and
inserted that into their tied yarn bunch. After a little

more tying, winding, and cutting, they each had a finished yarn doll!

"Cute! That was easy to do," said Kendall. "What
about eyes?"

"I have lots of buttons and ribbons in my sewing box.
You can glue buttons on for the eyes and dress her up
with a few ribbons if you would like," said Grandma.

"Grandma, this is fun," said Megan. "Can you teach
us how to make other stuff?"

"I'd love to. We have all summer to play together. I
have an idea about something we can do tomorrow. We
can use some of that sand and a few of the shells you
brought back from the beach today."

That night as Megan fell asleep, she thought about the
fun she had today, swimming at the beach, helping
Grandpa fish, collecting shells, and making the pretty
yarn doll. She thought about the lovely rag doll they had
found in the big box and opened her eyes to see the doll
resting comfortably in a small chair against the wall. She
smiled as she remembered the funny stories Grandpa
and Grandma told them about their mothers when they
were girls, and just before she dropped off to sleep, she
glanced at the table beside her bed. Yes, it was still there,
just where she had left it - - the key!

The next day was filled with activities that kept
Kendall and Megan busy all day long. Grandma taught
them how to make sand candles. They colored the wax
by melting old crayons they found upstairs in a cupboard and pressed their largest shells into the damp
sand, leaving a shell-shaped hole. Then they poured the
melted wax into the hole, one at a time, and made red

candles and blue candles and yellow candles, each one shaped like a real shell. It was wonderful fun. They each made candles for their parents and for friends back home. In the afternoon the girls both wrote long letters home telling of the fun they were having. Then they helped Grandpa in the garden pulling weeds. By dinner time, they were both exhausted, and neither one had thought about their treasures upstairs in the blanket chest, the old letters, or the secret key.

After dinner Grandma said, "Do you want to read more of your old letters? Why don't you go upstairs and get them. Let's see what else we can find out about the girl who wrote them."

The girls climbed the stairs to the blanket chest in the hallway. "Is the key safe?" asked Kendall in a whispered voice.

"Yeah, I was keeping it on the table next to my bed, but I decided it was safer to keep it with me, see," she said as she fished out a piece of yarn that was tied around her neck. Suspended on the length of yarn was the key.

"Good idea. Megan, we have to figure out a way to get back to that museum without Grandpa getting suspicious. We need to get our box back so we can try out the key. You're good at figuring out stuff. Got any ideas?"

"No, not yet, but I'm thinking. I'll let you know when I come up with something." She was pleased that Kendall looked to her for a solution to their problem.

Back downstairs Grandma carefully unfolded the third letter and read it aloud.

March 7, 1810

My Dear Cousin Anah,

I am glad the winter is nearly over. This morning, Daniel and I made a broom from a branch of the old birch tree by the barn. Then he worked on a butter paddle he is making for Mother. I spent the rest of the day making candles. Daniel and I collected wax myrtle berries for them yesterday. Mother boiled the berries then I dip them 25 times for them to be strong enough. What a chore!

In the evenings I have been practicing my stitching. Grandmother Watson is teaching me to quilt and told me I must endeavor to be diligent. I try to make my stitches small and even but I need to practice a lot more before they look as nice as Grandmother's beautiful stitches! I am making a small quilt for cousin Dorothy.

Tomorrow is wash day. I hope it is warm again. Soon we will be working in the garden . Spring is in the air. Then comes summer and I will be able to visit with you again. I hope you and your family are well.

    Your cousin,

    Eliza Edmonds

    P.S. I am bringing a special friend with me when I visit! I hope you like her.

CHAPTER 6
THE DIARY

The next morning the girls both slept in late. They had just come downstairs when Grandpa came in through the screen door on the porch. "A couple of sleepy heads this morning, I see. Well, I have a letter here from 12 Dorset Lane in Mill Valley. Sound familiar?" asked Grandpa.

"That's for me! It's from Mom!" Megan squealed as she recognized the handwriting on the letter. She quickly tore open the envelope and pulled out the letter. She read it through then folded it back up and tucked it inside the envelope. "Mom and Dad are fine. Dad is busy working on Mom's new office at night. Dad's brother, Uncle Paul, is visiting and he's helping Dad. It's going well and it'll be finished sooner than he thought. And Mom said her new book is coming along great and she thinks it will be done pretty soon, too. They said they might come back here to Virginia later on this summer while I'm still here. Isn't that great!" exclaimed Megan excitedly.

"That would be wonderful," said Grandma as she walked out of the kitchen. "This old house loves company. I'll call your mother this evening and see what their plans are."

"It would be great to have your parents here, Megan. Your mom hasn't been here in years, and your dad is very handy and I could use some help around this place. These old houses always need work. Kendall, maybe we can get your parents and your brothers down here, too? What do you think about that?" asked Grandpa.

"Oh, I don't think they have the time for a vacation this summer, Grandpa. Mom is really busy at work and the boys are at camp, and Dad doesn't even have time to come home. Maybe some other time, though, okay? It would be fun to have everyone together sometime," replied Kendall.

"Well, I thought we ought to bring those letters of yours over to the museum today. The curator said he would like to look at them, remember?" said Grandpa.

They girls looked at each other in surprise. "Great idea, Grandpa!" said Kendall. "We can be ready to go as soon as you want."

"Have some breakfast and then we can go. I'll be out on the porch reading."

"Girls, these letters are extraordinary. They're very well preserved. The ink is still plenty dark enough to read. I'd like to be able to spend more time reading them. May I copy them? Then I'll give them back to you for safekeeping. I'll just run upstairs and copy them now if you don't mind."

The girls waited as Mr. Parks, the museum curator, walked up the stairs. Grandpa glanced out the window and said, "Oh, there's Henry. I haven't seen him in ages. I'll be right back."

As their grandfather went out the door, Kendall

turned to Megan. "Now's our chance. You have the key, don't you?"

"Sure, it's right here," and she pulled the key from around her neck.

"Good, because our box is over there on the table and I think we should see if the key fits it."

The girls hurried over to their wooden box. Kendall picked it up as Megan started to insert the key into the keyhole. Just then, they heard footsteps on the stairs.

"Here you go, girls. All copied and these are yours to keep. Just please be very careful with them."

Kendall quickly set the box back down and Megan shoved the key, yarn and all, into her pocket. "Oh, thanks. We'll be very careful with them. We haven't even finished reading them all yet. Our grandmother is helping us because they're kind of hard to read," explained Kendall.

"I'll put these copies in our archives. We have a pretty extensive collection of materials from the early 1800s, but you girls have found a number of objects that we would love to add to our collection. We can discuss the possibilities of putting your collection here at the museum at another time. Where's Warren?"

"Grandpa is outside talking to a friend. Umm, when do you think we can have the rest of our stuff back?" asked Megan hesitantly.

"Are you in a rush? I thought you girls were going to be here all summer!"

"Well, it's just that we wanted to, um, show them to some friends. Actually, if we could just have our little box, then you can keep the other things as long as you need to," stammered Megan.

"I suppose that would be alright. Just be extremely

careful with that box, okay?" said the curator.

"Oh, yes, we will," said Megan with a smile.

"We sure will," agreed Kendall.

The girls said their goodbyes and hurried outside to meet their grandfather.

"I see you have your little box back. Was Mr. Parks finished looking at it?" asked Grandpa.

"I guess so. And he copied the letters so we have our letters back, too. He's keeping the other stuff for a little while longer," said Kendall hurriedly.

"Then I guess we can go home. Do you girls have plans for today?" asked Grandpa.

"Well, Grandma has another project for us this afternoon that sounds like fun. But first we have been wanting to just take a walk around. We haven't really had time to do much of that yet," answered Megan.

"It's a pretty day for a walk, that's for sure. I'll drop you two off at the house, then I have some errands to run."

"Thanks, Grandpa," the girls said together.

After quickly putting their letters on the table just inside the front door, Megan and Kendall walked down the street past their grandparents' house, looked around, then ran back to the house and rushed into the backyard, past the old barn, and sat down on a fallen log far behind the house.

"I thought we would never get this box back," said Kendall as she held the box firmly on her lap.

"Me too, but I'm almost afraid to try the key. What if it doesn't fit?" asked Megan nervously.

"Just try the key, then we'll know, okay?"

Megan pulled the key out of her pocket and with a

shaking hand, inserted it into the keyhole on the front of
the box. "It fits!"

"Turn it and see if we can open this up."

Megan tried to rotate the key in both directions without success. "It doesn't turn, and I'm afraid to push too
hard. I don't want to break it."

"Here, let me try," said Kendall. She held the key
firmly and tried to twist it back and forth. "It's moving a
little, I think. Oh!" she gasped as the key turned in the
old lock.

"Open it," cried Megan breathlessly.

Kendall slowly, carefully raised the lid.

"Ahhh!" The girls stared silently into the small box.

There it was, a small, hand stitched book. *"My Diary"*
was carefully written on the cover.

"Amazing! I can't believe this. I'm almost afraid to
touch it," said Megan.

"We'll be careful. It's ours, so we can touch it if we
want." Kendall reached into the box and gently lifted out
the small book. She opened the cover and on the first
page was carefully written:

Steal not this book, for if you do,

The devil will be after you.

Locked in my box I will keep,

This treasured book while I sleep.

Around my neck I keep my key,

Far from the prying eyes of thee!

Anah Matthews

"This is her book, the same Anah that those letters are written to. I can't believe it! It's so old, but it still looks almost new," said Megan. "What are we going to do with it, Kendall?"

"We're going to read it, silly, and we can figure out what to do with it later."

"Should we show it to Grandma? She could help us read it!" suggested Megan.

"No way. This is going to be our secret. At least for now, anyway."

"Then we're going to have to hide it. Where should we keep it?" Megan asked.

"Locked in the box, just like the book says. 'Locked in my box I will keep this treasured book while I sleep. Around my neck I keep my key, far from the prying eyes of thee!' And you've already been keeping the key around your neck. This is almost creepy, don't you think?" asked Kendall as the two girls huddled together and began reading the handwritten pages.

"So what were you three ladies doing this after-noon?" asked Grandpa.

"Grandma taught us how to print using soap," said Megan excitedly.

"Print with soap? How does that work?"

"Well, we used bars of soap and carved out designs with the vegetable peeler. Then we used a small sponge and wiped paint over the top of the bar of soap, and the paint stays on the part of the design that hasn't been cut away. Then we just turned the soap over and pressed it onto paper. It's really cool. We put them on the back porch to dry. We'll show you after dinner," Kendall explained.

"That's great. Sounds like fun. So what else do you have planned for these girls while they're here, Elizabeth?"

"Oh, I have plenty of ideas to keep them busy. I've been planning for months. But this afternoon I thought of something that you girls might want to learn about. Remember when we were reading your old letters and you wanted to know who all the people are who are mentioned in the letters? Well, I was thinking about that and thought you might want to learn a little bit about genealogy."

"What's that?" asked Megan.

"It's the study of families. Some people call it family trees. You use genealogy to learn about your family, or another family, generations and generations back. I thought we could draw a family tree for our family, at least as far back as I know, then as we read the letters, we can try to figure out who the people are and maybe we can make up a family tree for them. It could be fun, and a little like solving a mystery What do you think?" Grandma asked.

"That sounds neat! I love mysteries. How do we start?" asked Megan with a wide smile.

An hour later they had drawn out a family tree that showed Grandma and Grandpa and their own parents and grandparents above them. Below them were their three children, (Megan's and Kendall's mothers and the girls' Uncle Robert) and their grandchildren (Megan, Kendall and her two brothers, and Uncle Robert's two children).

"That was pretty easy! Now, what about your grand-parents' parents?" asked Megan.

"I don't know much more about our family than this. It would be interesting to know, though. This house first belonged to Grandpa's grandfather, Thomas Bayley. And it's stayed in the family ever since. I suppose I could do some research at the library and see what other information I can find. There must be records some-where."

"Where do we start with a family tree for our let-ters?" asked Kendall.

"Well, that's going to be more difficult. We'll have to go back over the letters and make a list of each person that's mentioned and then try to fit them together, kind of like a puzzle." Megan and Kendall looked at eachother and smiled. "It's getting too late to start on that tonight, but we can work on it tomorrow if you want. Now, go on upstairs and get ready for bed. We'll be up in a few minutes to tuck you in.".

"Did you girls enjoy your walk?" asked Grandpa as the girls started up the stairs.

"Walk? Oh, yeah, our walk! It was nice!" answered Kendall as the girls scooted up the stairs.
"That was close! Megan, bring the diary into my room after Grandma and Grandpa come up so we can read some more. I have the flashlight!"

April 2, 1809

Collected berries with James and John. It should be enough for ink for us all for a long time. I will practice my writing to please Mother.

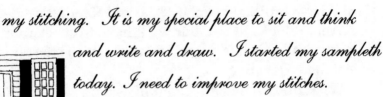

April 6, 1809

    Warm weather today. Sat
outside on the steps and worked on
my stitching. It is my special place to sit and think

and write and draw. I started my sampleth
today. I need to improve my stitches.
Mother says they are too large. I will try
to slow down and work more carefully.

May 15, 1809

    Father brought us each a beautiful spoon today.
They have our initials engraved on them. They are
gifts from Mrs. Agnes Kerr. She was well pleased
with the chest Father made for her home. It was like
the chest Father made for
Mother when I was a baby
and painted the same blue
and white. I will find a
special place to keep my

*spoon. I will keep it for when I marry. Perhaps
Father will make a chest for me one day and I will
keep my special treasures there.*

"Look at her little drawing of a blanket chest. Do you
think that's our blanket chest?" asked Kendall excitedly.
"Well, it looks like it, but we'll have to check ours
more carefully. If it is ours, I wonder which chest it is?"
questioned Megan.
"What do you mean?" Kendall asked.
"Well, it looks like her father made one for Mrs. Kerr,
and one for her mother, and Anah was hoping that her
father would make one for her, too. So I wonder which
one ours is?" she questioned aloud. "But we don't know
if he actually ever made one for her. But because we
found all of this stuff together, I think that her father
probably made our chest for someone in her family and
they used it to store all their things in. So that eliminates
the chest that he made for Mrs. Kerr. Grandpa said that
he's going to try to find out who the blanket chest belonged to, or who put it into the auction. I bet it belonged to Anah's mother."
"Do you think the spoon she talks about is the same
spoon that we found?" asked Kendall.
"Well, Mr. Parks at the museum said that it probably
belonged to the person who made the sampler, remember? Because the initials were the same as Anah's. And
we know Anah made the sampler because she put her
name on it," answered Megan. "So that has to be her
spoon. I sure wish we knew more about who these

people were. Tomorrow, let's get some paper and try to figure out their family tree. We can look at the letters and write a list of all the names mentioned, and then add any more names we find in the diary. This is kind of like doing a jigsaw puzzle. We are finding some of the pieces in the letters and some of the pieces in the diary. We could ask Grandma to help us," suggested Megan.

"But Grandma doesn't know about the diary, remember? And I think that we should keep it a secret awhile longer. Okay?"

"Okay! I love secrets," said Megan.

"Can you believe this? This is so neat!" Kendall said as she carefully turned the pages of the small, old book. "And it's really cool that she drew some pictures in her diary."

"We should show this to Grandma. She would really like it," said Megan thoughtfully.

"Well, let's not tell her yet. Then we can show it to her and to Grandpa, too. We better get some sleep or we'll sleep all day tomorrow."

A few minutes later Megan was back in her room with the locked box tucked under her bed and the key safely around her neck. The last thing she saw before dropping off to a deep sleep was the old rag doll sitting peacefully on the little chair.

CHAPTER 7
JACK

Megan woke with a start the next morning and spoke to the old rag doll, "You aren't Nelly. You can't be. Eliza made Nelly, but you were in Anah's chest with her things. So who are you? And who made you?" She had been dreaming of Anah and Eliza all night and was trying to piece together the mystery. She needed more clues.

Downstairs at breakfast, Grandma said, "I talked to your mother, Megan, and she and your dad are planning to come for a visit later this summer. You girls will have to help me get another bedroom ready for them. Good thing this house is big enough for all the company we want. That's one nice thing about these old houses."

"That may be the reason they built this house. The old cottage was just too small for a growing family," said Grandpa.

"What old cottage?" asked Kendall.

"That's the little house back in the woods way beyond the barn. It hasn't been used for years. Your mothers used to play in it when they were kids, and I don't think anyone has been in it since. And no one's actually lived in it since this house was built, around 1900," explained Grandpa.

"You mean the cottage has been empty for over 100 years?" asked Megan.

"Yes, and it isn't in very good shape, but we haven't torn it down. Seems a shame to do that. So we just leave it be."

"I haven't seen a cottage back there. Where is it, Grandpa?" asked Megan.

"Can we go in it?" asked Kendall excitedly.

"You can't see it very well because of all the trees and weeds grown up around it. But it's back there, on the far side of our property. This used to be a farm, so it's a pretty deep piece of land. The cottage is probably locked. And I don't know how safe it is inside. But you can walk around the outside if it isn't too overgrown. I'm sure it was a pretty little place when it was built."

The girls were anxious to explore the little cottage, so Grandma packed them a picnic lunch in a basket and sent them out the back door. "I have another project for you girls for this afternoon, so come back in a few hours and we'll play," said Grandma.

They headed toward the barn, then past the fallen log, and kept walking. The grass ended and the trees and bushes became thick. It was impossible to walk in a straight path, as they had to wind their way through the dense brush.

"I hope we aren't lost," said Megan. "Where's this cottage? I thought it would be right here."

"It can't be much farther 'cause it's on Grandpa's property. We must be close."

The girls went several steps more then stopped. "Here it is!" cried Megan.

Right in front of them was a small house that was barely visible because of the thick vines, bushes, and trees. They set down their basket and walked closer. Underneath the heavy vines they could see a door, windows, and the remainders of black wooden shutters on either side of the windows. The windows were too high to look into, and besides, the glass was so covered with dust and grime that it was impossible to see inside. They tried to walk around the house but some of the bushes had thorns and that halted their attempt.

"We should come back here later and see if we can clear off some of these vines. I would love to see what this place looks like underneath all this stuff," said Kendall.

"Yeah, it's so cute. I can't believe my mom used to play here and never even told me about it," marveled Megan.

"My mom played here, too, and she never said anything to me about it either. I wonder why?" asked Kendall.

The girls poked around the front of the house a bit longer, then found a cleared space just a short distance away. "We can have our picnic right here," announced Megan. "And I brought the diary. I stuck it in the basket just before we left. Let's read some more and see what else we can find out, okay?"

The girls sat close together munching their sandwiches while they deciphered Anah's old-fashioned handwriting:

July 6, 1809

     Today I finally finished my sampleth and added the date. It took a very long time to com-

plete! Mother is pleased with my work, which makes me very happy. James and John went fishing in the creek and caught 9 fish! They were very excited! Very hot today.

October 3, 1809

I received a letter from cousin Eliza. She has seen our new cousin, baby Dorothy. Daniel is still busy whittling! Eliza will visit again in the spring. I cannot wait to see her. We always have such fun together. Mother baked apples today! Father is busy working on a house in town and many people are waiting for him to make presses for them. He is very tired every night.

December 30, 1809

We had a light snowfall yesterday. It was beautiful. Father finished the cradle he has been making for me! He made it in the evenings and let me help him. It is very pretty and I will keep it in my room by my bed. I cannot wait to show it to Eliza, as she is making a baby and will love seeing a cradle for it. I am going to make a little blanket for the cradle.

February 21, 1810
          Another letter from cousin Eliza! They are having more snow in Maryland than we are here. I have a surprise for Eliza. I will give her my cradle for the baby she is making! And I will try to finish the blanket I am making for the cradle. Father thinks that it is a good and generous plan. John lost his hornbook for two days, then found it under the stairs! Mother was furious!

"What was that?" asked Megan.
"What? I didn't hear anything."
"I heard a funny noise!" said Megan.
"It's probably some kind of bird or something. Keep reading!"

March 10, 1810

Father showed me the secret hiding place he made. It fits the same key as my special box.   He said we can hide things there when we travel to visit Grandmother and Grandfather Matthews next month. I can use it to hide my treasures. I put my spoon inside, and will keep my letters from Eliza hidden as well. James and John do not know about the secret door! They only know that I treasure my clothespress and do not understand why!

March 30, 1810

I received a letter from Aunt Mary Watson. Baby Dorothy is very healthy and doing well. Her three brothers are helping Aunt Mary a great deal. Aunt Mary would like to come for a visit sometime and I would love to see her. I received another letter from cousin Eliza. I cannot wait for her to visit. I will show her the secret of my clothespress and will give her the cradle! She will come with her family in the spring for a visit. It has been a long winter and I look forward to having a friend my own age to visit with!

June 2, 1810

Cousin Eliza and Daniel left yesterday. I was sad to see them leave. We had a lovely visit. I told Eliza about the clothespress. She loved the secret! We did not let the boys know about it! She gave me a beautiful baby that she made. She has named her Nelly and I will call her that, too.

She worked on Nelly all winter as a surprise for me! I gave her the cradle that Father and I made, and the blanket that I stitched. She was quite pleased with her gifts. I wish that Eliza lived closer so that we could be together more often. We have great fun together!

"There! I heard it again!"

"Megan, I'm sure there are all kinds of birds and squirrels and things out here. We're in our own backyard. There's nothing else out here but us and a few birds. Keep reading."

"Did you see this? Eliza gave her Nelly, so the rag doll we found really must be the one that Eliza made. Now we know how it got to the chest with the rest of Anah's things. That's one mystery solved," said Megan with satisfaction.

June 14, 1810

James and his friend, Thomas, tried to read my diary. I will have to hide it in my box always! I do not know why Thomas has to be here so often. He and James are always together. They have been teasing me and making me angry! I wish

*they would go away and stop
bothering me!*

July 10, 1810
*I received a letter from Eliza. She and her family
arrived home safely. She thanked me again for the
cradle. Our garden is lovely this summer. We
have so many vegetables that we can give some to
our neighbors. I spent the day weed-
ing the garden. James and his friend
Thomas picked berries. Mother and
I will make preserves this week. Tomorrow we will pick the geese for new
quills. John has a new knife and will
teach me to cut my own quills. I need
a special quill for drawing.*

September 2, 1810
*Thomas' father is sick so I helped Thomas with his
chores today. We cut potatoes for his sheep, watered*

the horses, churned butter, and gathered wood for the fire. He will help Father in the evenings with the presses and chests he is making. Father is so busy all the time. People stop by often to admire his work. It keeps him so busy, I am glad Thomas can help him.

"I definitely heard something that time. Didn't you hear it?" asked Megan.

Before Kendall could answer, their attention was drawn to the sound of cracking branches behind them.

"Hide the diary," whispered Kendall.

"What are you guys doing?" asked the boy as he reached the clearing. He was wearing shorts and a tee shirt and appeared to be about their age. He had a large wooden whistle hanging around his neck.

"Who are you? And what are you doing here?" said Kendall boldly.

"My name's Jack, and I live down the street from your grandparents. Your grandmother told me you two were back here. So what did you just shove into the basket?"

"None of your business. We're having a picnic and I don't think you were invited," said Kendall.

"Well, I could leave, but then I'd have to tell your grandmother that you two are hiding something, and she might start asking questions. Or, you could show me what you're hiding, and I'll keep my mouth shut! Your choice!"

The girls looked at each other in shock. They hadn't planned on sharing their secret with anyone yet, and especially not with a stranger.

Kendall spoke right up. "We aren't hiding anything. I have a letter from a friend from home and we were just reading it, that's all. You wouldn't be interested in it; it's girl stuff. She's complaining about her two younger brothers who are away at camp this summer. And her mother makes her do lots of the housework and even some of the cooking. Boring stuff, trust me." Kendall winked at Megan, who returned the wink!"

"Camp, huh? What kind of camp?" asked Jack.

"It's a wilderness camp with canoeing, hiking, building campfires, you know, that kind of camp."

"Sounds great! I just got back from camp myself last night. It was awesome! We canoed and went swimming and played baseball, and did all kinds of cool stuff. I wish I could have stayed all summer but I could only stay for a week. My best friend, Brian, is there for the whole summer. Man, he's so lucky. There aren't too many kids around the neighborhood, especially around my age. Mostly it's me and Brian hanging out together. We have a band!" revealed Jack triumphantly.

"You do? What kind of a band?" asked Megan.

"You know, a rock band. I play the guitar and Brian plays the drums. We're pretty good. We're working on a name for the band. Right now we call ourselves 'Weasels on Skateboards' because when we aren't practicing for the band, we're skateboarding! Pretty cool, huh?"

"Yeah, I guess." The girls exchanged puzzled looks.

"What do you have around your neck?" Megan asked shyly.

"This? It's a whistle, silly." Jack blew on the whistle and it made a funny bird-like sound. "I made it myself," Jack answered as he reached into his pocket and pulled out a small penknife.

"That's really cool!" exclaimed Megan.

"Okay, listen, I'm sorry. I didn't mean to scare you or anything when I walked up. I know that you two have been here in town for only a week. You don't have to show me anything. I just wanted to come over and say, 'hi'."

The girls relaxed a bit. "I'm sorry, too. I wasn't very nice when I told you to leave. It's just that it's a little spooky out here by this old house. And we haven't met any other kids here. I'm Kendall. And this is my cousin, Megan."

"Hi."

"Hi. So, what do you girls know about this old place? I've never been out here before. I actually didn't even know it was here."

"Well, our grandfather said that it's belonged to his family for a long time. In about 1900, they built a bigger house, the one my grandparents live in now. I don't know how old this little house is, but Grandpa said no one has lived here for over 100 years."

"Neat! This place would look really cool if it was cleaned up. You want some help pulling off these vines?" asked Jack.

The girls looked at each other questioningly, then smiled. "Sure, that would be great. It's going to be a big job, and we could really use some help," said Kendall.

"I think we should use gloves and we need clippers and stuff like that. I have some at my house. Do you want to meet back here later and get started?" asked

Jack.

"Yeah, that would be great! We have to go back to the house and talk to Grandma first. Why don't we meet back here in about an hour?" said Kendall.

"Okay! See you guys later," said Jack as he turned and walked away.

"He seems nice. But I'm glad he didn't see the diary. I'm not ready to show it to anyone yet," said Megan.

"Yeah, he did seem nice, and it would be great to have someone else to help us pull off these vines. Then maybe we could go inside the cottage and look around."

The girls picked up their basket and walked toward their grandparents' house.

"There are a bunch of words in the diary that I don't know, like hornbook and clothespress. What do you think was the secret about the clothespress? And I don't know what she meant about cutting quills. I wish we could ask Grandma about them," said Megan.

"We will, but just not now. I have been thinking about that clothespress thing. She talks about a secret door and using the same key, and she's going to put stuff in there. Seems to me that a clothespress has something to do with pressing clothes, you know, like ironing. Maybe she is talking about an iron or an ironing board?"

"But how would an iron have a secret door on it that you could open up and hide things in?" questioned Megan.

"I don't know, but maybe they used a different kind of iron back then? Maybe it was a lot bigger? We'll have to figure that part out. Maybe Mr. Parks can help us with that. Meanwhile, we need to start a list of the people that Eliza named in her letters and that Anah has in her diary. We know that they're cousins, so maybe we can start working on their family tree," said Kendall. "That might help us figure this all out."

CHAPTER 8
THE COTTAGE

 The girls had checked in with Grandma, changed into long pants and long-sleeved shirts, and Grandpa had helped them gather gloves and gardening tools to take back to the cottage. Grandpa was pleased that they were so interested in the little cottage. He hadn't seen it himself in years, and planned to take a walk back there later in the afternoon to see it.

As the girls headed back to the cottage, they could hear music off in the distance. When they arrived at the little house, Jack was already there, music blaring, busy yanking at vines from around the front steps and the door.

"Hey! Dig in. There's plenty to go around," he called with a grin as he turned down the music.

"Oh, this stuff is unbelievable. We'll never get it all off," said Kendall.

"It's not that bad. It pulls off pretty easily. But we need to be careful, especially around the windows and shutters. I don't want to break anything. Just start pulling and the stuff unwraps itself. It isn't that hard."

Several hours later the three were near exhaustion and stopped to rest. "We made a lot of progress. You can see the whole front of the house. I don't know how sturdy these steps are, but we could try to go in. I wonder why the house has two front doors and a chimney at either end. Really cool place."

Just then, Grandpa appeared in the clearing. "Oh my gosh! You kids have worked a miracle here. Just look at this place. I haven't seen it in years, it was so covered with vines and weeds. This is fantastic. I'll have to bring your grandmother out here. She'll love to see the old place. We haven't been out here since your mothers were children. And I found the old key. It's been hanging on a nail on the back porch for ages."

Grandpa showed the three children a very large, heavy key.

"Wow! What a cool key. That's for this house?" asked Jack.

"Sure is. This key has to be 150 years old at least. I don't know when this little house was built, but it's pretty old. Well, why don't you kids rest a little longer, and I'll go back to the house and get your grandmother and bring back something cool for you to drink. Then, we'll see if we can open up the house. How does that sound?"

"That would be great, Grandpa," said Kendall.

"Yeah, that would be terrific, Mr. Bayley. I'd do just about anything for a glass of water."

"I can't wait for Grandma to see how much we've done," said Megan.

"We'll be right back, then," said Grandpa as he turned and disappeared into the heavy brush.

"This is such a cool old place," sighed Jack. "You guys are so lucky that no one tore it down. I don't think my family has any place like this, and my mom would know. She's traced back our family for generations."

"Really? So you know about stuff like family trees?" asked Megan.

"Oh, yeah, my mom is nuts about genealogy. She's traced our family back to my great, great, great, I don't know how many greats grandfather. A guy named Joshua Walker. Then she kind of lost the trail, and has been stuck. She can't find any more information that goes back farther than that, but that guy, Joshua Walker, was born in 1795. Amazing, huh?"

"1795! That's so cool!" said Megan. She looked questioningly at Kendall, who returned the questioning look, then they both slowly nodded and smiled. "Jack, we're trying to do a little family tree ourselves. Do you think you might be able to help us?"

"Sure. You mean you're tracing back your own family? I bet your grandparents could help you with that. They would know a lot more than me."

"Not exactly. We did do a family tree of our family with our grandmother, but this is for another family. It's actually for a, well, for a friend who lived a long time ago," said Kendall. Megan nodded in agreement.

"Okay, what are you two talking about? A friend who lived a long time ago? What did you do, meet a ghost or something?" asked Jack with a smirk.

"First, before I tell you anything about this, you have to promise not to tell anyone. I mean not one person. Do you promise?" asked Megan.

Jack was intrigued. With Brian gone for the summer, who was he going to tell? "Sure, I promise," he said.

"Well, here's the story," said Megan. "We bought this box at an auction last week, and there was a bunch of really old stuff inside, and there were old letters, too. So we've been reading the letters and there are people in the letters and we want to figure out who they were."

"So that's what you were reading when I came here earlier," said Jack.

"Well, kind of. You see, we also found an old diary, and there are more people in the diary," explained Kendall.

"Cool! So you got a box at an auction with letters and a diary? That's awesome! I've been to a bunch of auctions but haven't ever found anything like that. I bet your grandparents were excited, too, huh?"

"Well, our grandparents don't know about the diary yet. We had this wooden box, and it was locked, and we took it to the museum, and then we moved a blanket chest that Grandpa bought at the auction, and we heard something rattling inside, and the man at the museum said that sometimes old chests have a false bottom, and we found the false bottom, only Grandpa said not to look for it, and we found a key inside the false bottom and it opened up the box and we found the diary inside," Megan said in one long breath.

"Unbelievable! You have a blanket chest with a false bottom. And there was a key inside? This is too much. So, where's the diary?" asked Jack.

"It's back at the house right now. But we'll show it to you later if you want."

"No kidding! I can't wait to see it. Let's use the old key and open her up. And, yeah, I'll help you with the family tree. My mom might even help us. I could ask her. She loves that stuff."

"That would be great," said Megan.

"Unbelieveable. This place looks just like it did when your mothers were girls," exclaimed Grandma. "Well, Warren, let's get the key and open her up."

Grandpa carefully climbed the wooden front steps and inserted the huge key into the heavy lock. It easily unlocked. He gave a strong push and the door swung open.

"Gosh," whispered Megan. "It looks like people still live here."

"Yes, I had forgotten that there was still furniture in here. I guess we just locked it up years ago and kind of forgot about it," said Grandpa.

"This place is so neat!" said Kendall.

Jack stood there with his mouth hanging open. "Cool," is all he could manage to say.

"We should be careful walking around here. I don't know how sturdy the floors are. I'd hate to find out the hard way that we have a weak floor. It's starting to get late. Let's head back to the house and have something to eat. Jack, would you like to join us for dinner?" asked Grandpa.

"Yeah, sure, thanks Mr. Bayley. I'll call my mom."

"Tomorrow we can come back out and see what work needs to be done. I want to make sure there aren't any loose floorboards or anything. I don't want anyone to get hurt out here," Grandpa said as he turned and headed to the door. "Great place. I had forgotten all about this place until this morning. Hmmm, I have an idea. Come on, kids. Let's get back to the house and we can talk about it."

"It would be a lot of work, but it'd be fun. What do

you think?" asked Grandpa.

"I think it's a great idea, Grandpa. And my dad can help when he gets here, too," said Megan.

"Warren, I think it's a fabulous idea," said Grandma. "I would love to see the cottage all fixed up. There's no reason not to. And the girls are here all summer. They'll be a big help."

"And I can help, too, if you want," said Jack.

"Well, Jack, we accept. I could really use your help," said Grandpa with a smile.

"This is the perfect project for the summer," said Kendall. "Just like the people in our letters. It'll be hard work, but fun, too. When can we start?"

"I'll look it over in the morning and then get a few men over to help me figure out where to start. You know, there's no water or electricity out there, so we'll really have a lot of work to do. We'll have to hire some people to do some of the work, but I think we can do a lot of it ourselves. It isn't in as bad shape as I thought it would be."

"Remember, I'll help as much as you want," said Jack. "Well, I better go home now. Thank you for dinner, Mrs. Bayley. See you two tomorrow?" asked Jack.

"Yeah. Maybe we can come over to your house? I'd like to meet your mom," said Kendall with a wink.

"Oh, sure. Come on over after breakfast. See you tomorrow."

"Bye, Jack," called Megan as he walked down the front steps.

Chapter 9
Family Tree

 "So, I understand you girls want to draw up a family tree, is that right?" asked Mrs. Walker, Jack's mother.

"Yes, and we have some of the names here, but we don't know too much about the people. We just know the names of two girls, and some of their family, and a friend," answered Kendall.

They were sitting with Jack at his kitchen table. His mother had set out several large sheets of paper and some pencils.

"We have a list of everything we know so far right here," said Megan. She pulled out the list that she and Kendall had written that morning and showed her list to Mrs. Walker.

"Well, this is a good start. I understand that you found some old letters at an auction. How wonderful. Genealogy can be lots of fun. Since this isn't your own family, we won't be able to ask your grandmother or anyone else questions about relatives. We're going to have to do some detective work, I imagine. We'll have to look for clues wherever we can find them. Think of this as a big puzzle. We'll start with the people we know. Eliza Edmonds and Anah Matthews. And you said the letters are dated 1809 and 1810? Do you know how old the girls are in the letters?" asked Mrs. Walker.

"No, they don't talk about birthdays. But we know they're cousins."

"Okay, that's fine. If they are cousins, then they have parents that are related, brothers or sisters. And they would have the same grandparents, at least on one side, just like you girls. Is there any mention of parents names or grandparents?"

"Yes. They talk about Grandmother and Grandfather Watson and an Aunt Mary and Uncle Hutchinson, and a baby cousin named Dorothy."

"Is Dorothy the sister of either of the girls, Eliza or Anah?" asked Mrs. Walker.

"No, I don't think so. I think she is just their cousin."

"So, the grandparents had at least three children, then. And Eliza's mother and Anah's mother were sisters."

"How do you know that?" asked Megan.

"Because Eliza and Anah have last names that are different from their grandparents'. The last name follows the son, but a daughter always changed her last name when she married. It's different today. Sometimes when women get married, they keep their last name and sometimes they change it to their husband's name. It's certainly going to make this kind of detective work harder in the future," said Mrs. Walker with a smile. "Was anyone else mentioned?"

"Yes, Eliza talked about her brother, Daniel. And she talked about seeing Anah and Aunt Elizabeth and Uncle Edwin and Anah's brothers," added Kendall.

"Hmmm, let's see now." Mrs. Walker was drawing lines on the paper and adding names. She was making notes down the side of the long sheet of paper. "So,

Anah's mother was named Elizabeth Watson until she married Edwin Matthews. Anyone else?"

"Eliza talked about an Uncle Richard who stayed with Grandma and Grandpa Watson."

"Okay. So maybe the Watsons had four children," Mrs. Walker said to herself as she erased a line and added another. "Any more people that you know about?" she asked.

"I think that Anah's two brothers were named James and John. She talked about doing chores with them and they caught nine fish on the day she finished her sampler," added Megan with excitement.

"Oh, I wish we could know what that sampler looked like. They always had dates on them and that would have helped us with the timeline for this family tree," said Mrs. Walker wistfully.

"We do have the sampler. And it has a date on it. She finished making it on July 6, 1809," answered Megan with glee.

"My word. You have the sampler? I can't believe it," said Mrs. Walker. "Well, now this is really getting exciting. And the sampler can give us a rough idea of Anah's age. Young girls, as young as eight years old, made their samplers. What other information do you have? Any details that were mentioned in the letters might be clues."

"The only other person I can remember is a friend named Thomas, but I don't know what his last name is. He is a friend of Anah's brother, James."

"This is a lot of information and we have quite a start on a family tree here, ladies. What I would like you to do is go back over your letters again very carefully. Write down any other details mentioned, any names,

dates, any places, anything else that you think might
help us figure out who these people were. Remember,
you have to be detectives looking for clues anywhere you
can!"

"Thank you, Mrs. Walker. We'll read them again and
see if we can get more clues for you," said Kendall.

"And we'll bring over the sampler for you to see. It's
really pretty."

"That would be wonderful. I'd love to see it. I enjoy
doing this, girls, so you stop by any time with any clues
you find, alright?"

"Okay, we will. Jack, do you want to come over and
check on the cottage?"

"Yeah! 'Bye, Mom. Later."

"So where are you two hiding this diary?" asked Jack
as they walked to the Bayley's house.

"I'm keeping it just where Anah said to keep it. I
have it locked inside her box," replied Megan.

"You talk like you know this girl, Megan," said Jack.

"Well, I feel like I do a little bit. Don't you feel that
way, too, Kendall?" she asked shyly.

"Yeah. I feel like Anah and Eliza are friends of ours.
I feel some kind of connection to them. I know that
probably sounds weird, but that's how I feel. And I
really want to find out more about them," explained
Kendall.

"Me, too. I feel the same way. I even had a dream
about them the other night," added Megan.

"Oh, brother! You girls are nuts," said Jack.

"Well, if that's how you feel, then maybe you don't
want to see the diary," retorted Kendall.

"I was just kidding. I want to see it. I've never seen anything old like that and it sounds really cool. Too bad you didn't find a boy's diary, huh?"

"Yeah, sorry about that, Jack. But you have to promise not to tell anyone about this, okay? We want to keep it a secret for a while longer. We'll tell our grandparents about it later, but not now. It's more fun this way. And we'll show it to your mom later, too. She was a big help with the family tree. Megan, we need to read the rest of the letters and finish reading the diary and take notes from the other letters, too. I bet we missed some clues already that could help Jack's mom with the family tree," Kendall said.

"Hey, I can help you with the clues," said Jack.

"Okay, we can all three do it. That way maybe we won't miss anything important," said Kendall.

They were standing on the front porch of Grandma and Grandpa's house. "Megan, go get the diary and meet us by the big log, okay?" said Kendall.

Megan turned and hurried inside. They could hear her footsteps running up the stairs as they walked down the porch steps and headed for the backyard.

November 16, 1810

It is very cool and all the trees have already turned colors and lost most of their leaves. I received a letter from Eliza today. She has a new neighbor, Joshua. He and Daniel are friends. They are whittling birds together. I think Eliza likes Joshua! James and I helped Thomas with the barn he is building. Thomas is very good at building and he is quite funny. Father says Thomas is a great help to him building chests. I am glad Thomas is here to help Father. He works hard and is very strong. Also, Thomas is very nice to me!

"That's the last entry in the diary. I wonder where the rest is?" said Megan.

"It sounds like Anah likes Thomas. Hmmm, that's kind of cute, don't you think, Megan?" asked Kendall.

"Come on you two. Don't get all mushy on me. We're supposed to be looking for clues, remember?" said Jack.

"Well, I think it's nice. Hey, Megan, did you bring the rest of the letters?" Kendall asked.

"I looked for them on the sideboard where we left them the last time Grandma helped us read them. But they weren't there. I thought maybe you put them someplace."

"No. I haven't touched them. Oh, well, I think there was only one or two left anyway. We can read them later and see if there are any more clues that we need," said Kendall.

"I have some paper and a pen here in my pocket. Let's look at this diary and see if we can find anything that my mom needs to help us fill in your family tree," said Jack matter-of-factly.

CHAPTER 10
Clues

"You three have done some wonderful detective work here," said Mrs. Walker later that afternoon as she looked over their list of the information they found in the diary. "This will all be quite helpful to us. We're going to start to fill in the story about these people's lives. Aunt Mary and Uncle Hutchinson's last name was Watson. So Hutchinson Watson was the son of Grandfather and Grandmother Watson. And you said here that Anah's father made a blanket chest for a lady named Agnes Kerr?"

"Yes, that was in the d-, um, in a letter we found," said Kendall.

"Absolutely amazing. The Kerr family built a big, brick home here on the Shore. Their house is now a museum. You girls have been there, right?" asked Mrs. Walker.

"Oh, yes. Grandpa took us over there and we showed our stuff to Mr. Parks, the curator. He was pretty interested in everything. And he made copies of the letters, too," explained Kendall.

"Well, then, he knows about the Kerr connection if he saw these letters. I'm surprised he wasn't ecstatic when he read about Agnes Ker. This is an important piece of local history," said Mrs. Walker.

Megan realized that the information about Agnes Kerr was from the diary. Mr. Parks didn't know about the diary. At least, not yet!

"I'm not sure if he actually read the letters. He made a copy, but maybe he didn't actually read them," suggested Megan.

"Astounding, really. And you wrote here that Eliza lived in Maryland. Do you know the name of the town?" asked Mrs. Walker.

"No, we didn't see that anywhere," answered Megan. "By the way, what's a hornbook?"

"Well, a hornbook was a teaching tool for children who were learning to write. It had the alphabet on it for the children to copy. It was called a hornbook because the paper was mounted on a piece of wood and protected by a thin layer of horn that was almost clear. It was very important back then for children to practice good penmanship. Children took great pride in their carefully drawn letters. Not like today, unfortunately," said Mrs. Walker as she looked at her son.

"Oh, Mom," said Jack.

"We know that baby.Dorothy had three brothers, but we don't know their names," said Megan, reading from their list. "And Eliza made a baby for Anah. That's a doll, right?"

"That's right. Girls called their dolls babies back then," explained Mrs. Walker.

"And Anah's father made a cradle for Eliza's doll," added Kendall. "We found a doll cradle in our box from the auction."

"Astonishing. This is just incredible, girls," said Mrs.

Walker as she continued to write notes down the sides of her paper.

"Can we ask you a few more questions?" asked Megan.

"Of course."

"Can you tell me what it means to cut quills?" she asked.

"Well, I think you are talking about goose quills, right?" asked Mrs. Walker.

"I guess so," Megan replied.

"People plucked some of the feathers, or quills, from their geese. Then they used a knife to cut the quill at an angle to make a pen. They left the feathers on, and that is what they wrote with. Jack, you know that penknife you have?" asked Mrs. Walker.

"Yeah?"

"It's called a penknife because a long time ago, people used small knives like that to cut their quills to make pens. So they called them penknives. And we still call them that today. Interesting, huh?" asked Mrs. Walker.

"Neat. I didn't know that. That's really cool, Mom."

"I have one more question, Mrs. Walker. What's a clothespress?" asked Kendall.

"A press, any kind of press, was like a cupboard. A long time ago, houses didn't have closets. People needed a place to store their clothes, their dishes, their books, and so they used specially made cupboards called presses. A clothespress held clothes, a linenpress held bed linens, and a bookpress held books!"

"You mean, a clothespress isn't some kind of a thing you press clothes with?" asked Kendall.

"No, it's a cupboard, and usually a pretty large cup-

board, that held clothes. It would be something like a
wardrobe or an armoire, if you know what those are,"
explained Mrs. Walker.

Megan was busy thinking about what Anah had
written in her diary about the secret hiding place and the
secret door, and wondered what that had to do with a
clothespress.

"Mrs. Walker, thank you so much for helping us. We
might find a few more clues later, because we have
another letter or two to read. If we find out anything
important, we'll come back and tell you, okay?" said
Kendall.

"That's just fine. I'm enjoying this as much as you
kids are," said Mrs. Walker with a smile.

Back home, over a fresh fish dinner, the girls chatted
excitedly with Grandma and Grandpa about the little
cottage. Grandpa had several men lined up to help him
with a few big projects, like running electricity and water
out to the house and fixing the roof. But he wanted the
girls to help him start cleaning up the inside. They
planned to get started early the next morning.

"Grandma, have you seen our old letters?" asked
Megan as she helped to clear the table.

"Oh, yes, I forgot to tell you. Mr. Parks called and
asked if he could see them again. Apparently his copies
weren't clear enough and he wanted to read the original
letters. I hope you don't mind," said Grandma.

"That's fine. It's just that we were looking for them
and thought we lost them," explained Kendall.

"Well, they are safe and sound over at Kerr Place,"
said Grandma.

"Was Kerr Place Agnes Kerr's house before?" asked Megan.

"Well, yes it was. How did you know about Agnes Kerr?" asked Grandma with surprise.

"Uh, I think Jack's mom told us about her, right Kendall?" said Megan nervously.

"Oh, yeah, she did. She was telling us about, uh, about stuff that happened a long time ago. Did you know that penknives used to be for cutting goose quills to make pens?" said Kendall, quickly changing the subject.

"Very interesting. I didn't know that," said Grandpa. "What else did you learn?" asked Grandpa.

"Mrs. Walker told us about clothespresses. She said that a long time ago, houses didn't have closets and they made cupboards to keep their stuff in," explained Megan. "They called them presses and one for clothes was a clothespress and one for books was a bookpress. Neat, huh?"

"Very neat. As a matter of fact, we might have one of those presses out in the little cottage. We'll have to take a look when we go out their tomorrow," said Grandpa.

Megan flashed a look at Kendall. Another possible piece to their puzzle!

"I'll be up in a few minutes to tuck you two in. Go on upstairs and get ready for bed, girls," said Grandma.

"Close call, Megan. You almost blew it with that Agnes Kerr stuff," said Kendall when they got upstairs.

"I know it. I keep forgetting what we read in the letters and what we read in the diary," exclaimed Megan.

"I guess we better tell Grandma and Grandpa about the diary pretty soon. But we can wait a little bit longer, don't you think?" asked Kendall.

"Well, I guess so. But I better keep my mouth shut or I'm going to get us in trouble," she replied with a laugh as the girls headed for bed.

CHAPTER 11
THE LAST LETTERS

The next day the girls spent hours working at the little cottage. They started in the kitchen. They cleaned around the old fireplace and swept the wooden floor. Grandma brought damp rags for them to use on the windows. It was hard work!

Jack worked outside clearing away more of the brush surrounding the house. Grandpa and two other men had ladders up to work on the roof and were checking under the house. Grandma and Mrs. Walker brought lunch.

Early that evening, after long showers to wash off the dirt and grime, the girls were relaxing at the kitchen table, playing cards with Grandpa. Someone knocked at the door.

"Please come on in, Mr. Parks," they heard Grandma say.

"Good evening, Warren, ladies," said Mr. Parks as he followed Grandma into the kitchen. "I thought I would take a look at that blanket chest you told me about, Warren. Is this a good time? I hope I'm not interrupting."

"It's fine. The girls and I were just resting here after a busy day working on the old cottage out back. The chest is upstairs. Come on. I'm anxious for you to see it and tell me what you think," said Grandpa excitedly.

"This is definitely an old Eastern Shore piece," said Mr. Parks. "I can tell by the way it's built and by the type of wood. This is yellow pine. This is a very desirable piece for collectors of this type of Eastern Shore furniture. And the design of these panels is quite distinctive. They're reminiscent of the panels you find on old doors and paneled walls. In fact, that is what they are, in a manner of speaking. The man who made this chest was probably a carpenter who built houses. There weren't any furniture makers that we know of living here on the Shore at the time this was built, around the early 1800s, I'd say. The carpenters, or joiners, as they were called, made the furniture to go in the houses." Mr. Parks was on his hands and knees looking the chest over carefully. "I think there are some initials carved here on the bottom. Warren, can you tip this back while I take a closer look?" asked Mr. Parks. "E. M. Well, that was probably the initials of the man who made this chest."

The girls looked at each in silent knowledge. E.M. was the initials of Anah's father, Edwin Matthews! That meant that this was the chest Anah's father made for her mother, the one she had written about in her diary.

"I'm not familiar with any joiners of the time with those initials, but it's quite interesting. We have been researching this very topic and are trying to piece together a history of the men who built the houses and made the furniture as well. So far, we haven't come up with much definitive information, although we have made headway. It is difficult to track down information about people from so long ago. All we really have to go on is the estate records when someone dies. Perhaps your blanket chest will help us unravel the mystery of the joiners. I better be going," he said as he stood up. "Oh, I almost forgot. I have your letters in the car, girls. Let me get them for you. They are spectacular. I read them over today and made better copies. I would love to talk to you both sometime about those letters and the rest of the collection you found. I'll bring the rest of your objects by in the morning. I really appreciate the opportunity to study them."

Mr. Parks went to his car and returned with the letters. Megan and Kendall thanked him as Grandpa walked with Mr. Parks back to his car, talking excitedly about the old blanket chest.

"Grandma, we are really tired from working at the little house all day. We're going to go to bed now. See you in the morning," said Kendall as she and Megan headed for the stairs.

"Good night, girls. Sweet dreams."

A few minutes later, both girls were huddled together pouring over their stack of letters. There were five letters in all, so they had two more to read.

June 3, 1810

Dear Cousin Anah,

We arrived home safely from our visit with you and your family after a rather long journey. It was so wonderful to see you again. Thank you for the beautiful cradle you and Uncle Edwin made for me. I will make a new baby to sleep in it under the lovely blanket you sewed. I hope you are enjoying your new friend, Nelly!

I have always loved your house, but I especially enjoyed seeing the secret hiding place your father made in your bedroom. I love secrets! Thank you for sharing your secret with me. You can trust that I will tell no one!

Your cousin,

Eliza

October 28, 1810

My dear Anah,

The weather is cool today. I finished my chores early and am working on the quilt for Baby Dorothy. I need to finish it soon before she grows too big for it!

A new family moved to the next farm. They have only one son, a boy named Joshua.

*He is Daniel's age and they are already great
friends. Joshua is here at our home as much as my
own brother! Joshua loves to whittle as much as
Daniel does. We shall be buried under their birds
by spring if they whittle all winter! I shall tell you
a secret: I think Joshua Walker is very handsome
and kind!*

      Your cousin,

      Eliza

The girls stared at each other in shock!

"Joshua Walker? Could that be the same Joshua Walker that Jack said was his great, great, great grandfather? It can't be, can it?" asked Kendall.

"I don't know. Joshua Walker. Remember Jack said that he was born in 1795. This letter was written in 1810. So how old was this Joshua Walker in the letter?" Megan asked.

"Well, she said he was about the same age as Daniel, but we don't know how old Daniel was, do we? Oh, I wish we could figure this out. If it is the same Joshua Walker and if he was born in 1795, then he would be, um, oh, he would be 15 years old in 1810, right?" said Kendall.

"How did you figure that out?" asked Megan.

"Well, if he was born in 1795, then in 1800 he would be five years old, and in 1810 you add another 10 years, so that makes him 15," explained Kendall.

"Oh, yeah! So do you think Daniel was 15, too? How do we find out?" said Megan excitedly.

"I think we are going to have to show this to Jack, and then maybe to his mother. Mrs. Walker could figure this out for sure, don't you think?"

"Let's call Jack now, okay?" said Megan excitedly.

"We can't. It's too late, but we have to call him first thing in the morning. He's going to flip!"

CHAPTER 12
Secret Door

The girls were up and dressed early the next morning. They ate a quick breakfast and kept one eye on the clock. As soon as it was 9:00, they raced to the telephone.

"Hello, Mrs. Walker. It's Kendall Scott. Is Jack there? Oh, thanks," she said. "He's upstairs but she's going to get him," Kendall whispered to Megan. "Hi, Jack. It's Kendall. Listen, you have to meet us at the cottage right now! We have to talk to you. It's really important," she said excitedly. "Okay, we'll go there now and wait. See you in a few minutes," she said, then hung up the receiver.

"Is he coming?" asked Megan.

"Yeah, but he isn't ready yet. I told him we'd go out there now. Let's get the letters and the diary and go now," Kendall said.

"You girls are in quite a rush this morning," said Grandma as they were heading out the front door. "Where are you off to so early?" she asked.

"We're going out to the cottage to take a look around. We want to see how the work is coming," explained Megan.

"Okay, have fun," called Grandma as they raced down the porch steps and rounded the end of the house toward the backyard.

"Joshua Walker. I can't believe it! This must be the same guy, don't you think?" asked Jack after reading Anah's last two letters.

"We aren't sure, but we think so. Do you think your mother could find out?" asked Megan. The three children were sitting on the front steps of the old cottage, heads bent over the small, handwritten letter.

"My mom will go nuts when she reads this. This might be just the clue she has been looking for. Let me look at the diary again."

Megan handed Jack the diary. He flipped through the pages, searching for more clues. He stopped when he got to the page with the entry from April 6, 1809. He stared at the book, then turned to look at the door behind them. He shook his head in disbelief, then looked at the girls. "I can't believe this. Do you know where we are?" he said slowly.

"What do you mean, Jack? What did you see in the diary?" asked Kendall with growing excitement.

"I mean, we are sitting on Anah's steps, just like she was doing on April 6, 1809. This is her house, you guys! And this is her diary, and her letters, and everything," Jack explained incredulously.

"How do you know?" asked Megan, reaching for the diary.

"Here is her drawing of part of the front of her house. Look familiar?" he said, pointing to the house directly behind them.

"Oh my gosh. You're right! This is her house. And we know for sure that her father made the blanket chest we have at Grandpa's house," added Megan.

"What? You mean the one with the false bottom? How do you know that?" he asked.

"Because Mr. Parks came over last night and he found the initials E.M. on the bottom of the chest. He said it was made by a local carpenter. He didn't know any guys back then with those initials who made furniture, but we know from the diary that Anah's father built houses and made furniture. And his name was Edwin Matthews. It has to be him, don't you think?" she asked hopefully.

"It must be! And you know what this means, don't you?" he asked the girls.

"What?" asked both girls together.

"It means that the secret hiding place is inside this house! What are we waiting for? Let's go find it!"

All three children scrambled up the steps and through the unlocked door into the small cottage.

"Wait. The letters and the diary!" said Megan with a start. She ran back outside and gathered up their precious treasures.

"Hey, wait a minute. If we find this secret door, we need a key to open it. Do we have a key?" asked Jack quickly.

"I have it right here," announced Megan gleefully as she tugged on the yarn from around her neck. There, suspended on the yarn, was the key that opened the diary's box. "Anah said in her diary that the secret door uses the same key."

"Let's start here in the living room," said Kendall.

"No, remember, Anah said that the secret door is in her bedroom. And it has something to do with a clothespress. So where do you think her bedroom was?" asked Megan. "I don't remember seeing anything that looks like a bedroom when we were in here before."

Jack quickly ran out the front door and jumped down the steps to the ground. Then he turned and looked up toward the roof.

"What is it, Jack?" asked Kendall.

"There are windows up on the roof. That means there is a second floor to this house. I bet Anah's bedroom is upstairs," he said breathlessly as he ran back up the stairs and into the house. "Where is the staircase to go upstairs?"

"I don't know," Megan said.

"We have to find it. Let's start here and work our way to the other end of the house. Maybe it's hidden behind one of these big pieces of furniture or something. We have to find it," Jack pronounced.

The children searched each wall of the living room and peered behind each cupboard. They didn't find anything that looked like a stairway entrance. Then they moved into the kitchen. Again, they found nothing there. Disappointed, they stopped to catch their breaths. "Now what do we do?" asked Megan as she leaned up against the wall to the side of the fireplace. Just then, the wall moved slightly and Megan cried out, "Oh!"

"What's wrong, Megan?" asked Kendall with concern.

"I think I found a loose board on this wall. It scared me when I leaned against it, that's all. Grandpa said to be careful, and I guess this is what he meant."

"Let me see. Where did it move?" asked Jack as he quickly came to Megan's side.

"Right here. See? It's loose." She pushed on the board to show Jack how it moved, and just then there was a creaking sound and the whole large board swung forward. "Oh, my gosh. It's a door. We found the door! Come on."

The door swung out to reveal a small, winding stair-case that headed up. The children carefully climbed the stairs and found themselves in a small room with a slanted roof and one window.

"This is it!" cried Kendall excitedly. "This is Anah's bedroom."

Jack was busy exploring further and walked through another door and into a second bedroom. "Hey, guys, come in here. Here's another bedroom over here!"

"Well, one of these was Anah's room, and the other must have been for her brothers, Daniel, James and John, don't you think?" asked Megan.

"We are looking for a secret door, something that opens with a key. When we find that, then we'll know which room belonged to Anah. Remember that it has something to do with a clothespress. So it might be next to or behind one of the cupboards. Start looking. You guys start in this room and I'll look in the other one, okay?" said Jack.

The three started a careful search of each room. While looking inside one cupboard, Megan found sev-eral books. "Look! These must have belonged to our mothers, Kendall. I'll bet they played up here all the time. I remember my mom telling me how she loved reading mysteries when she was a girl. I'll bet these were hers. Hmmm, what's this? It's an old Bible. It sure looks old. Hey, look what's inside here. It's a family tree. Kendall, come here and look at this!" Megan read aloud, " 'Catherine Bell and Thomas Bayley, Jr.. Married 1838.' That's funny. Bayley is spelled the same as Grandma and Grandpa's last name."

"Grandpa said that there are lots of Bayley's here on the Shore. I think it's a pretty common name," said Kendall while she was continuing to search for the secret door.

"Let's see, it's a little hard to read this. Hmmm, I think they had three children, Adam, Rachel, and Elizabeth. And Adam was married to someone named Sarah in 1859. It looks like they had just one child, a boy named Edwin Bayley, who was born in 1862. It doesn't have anything else written after that." Megan turned the page and read on. "Wait, there's more. This shows Catherine Bell and Thomas Bayley's parents. Thomas' parents were Thomas Bayley, born in 1797 and, oh my gosh! Kendall, Jack, come here quick!! Thomas' mother was Anah Matthews, born in 1799. It's her, this is from Anah's family. I found it! Jack, Kendall, come and look at this!" shouted Megan excitedly.

The two joined Megan where she was jumping up and down and waving the old Bible in both hands.

"What did you find? What's so exciting? Show me, show me!" shouted Jack.

"This is the family tree from Anah's family. Look. Here she is, here's Anah, and here are her parents, Elizabeth Watson, born in 1780 and Edwin Matthews, born in 1778. They were married in 1799. And on this page it shows their children. I can't believe this!" Megan cried gleefully.

"Let me see that," said Kendall as Megan handed her the open book. "Anah Matthews, born in 1799, was married to Thomas Bayley, born in 1797. And they were married in 1817. Who did she marry? Oh no, do you think this is the same Thomas that's in her diary, the boy who tried to read her diary with her brother? And she married him? I can't believe this," said Kendall in disbelief.

"Hey, who cares who she married? We're supposed to be looking for the secret door, or did you two forget? Come on, let's bring the Bible back to your house later, but we have to find that door," said Jack.

The girls set the Bible down on a table and went back to their search for the secret door. All the while, though, they continued to talk about the newest clues they had found to Anah's family. "I can't believe this, Kendall. We've found her and even know about her children and grandchildren. All of a sudden she seems so old. I was used to thinking about her like a girl, just like us, but to read about her being married and having children, well, it's kind of strange, don't you think?" asked Megan.

Before Kendall could reply, Jack shouted to them from the other room in a muffled voice, "I found it, I found the door! Megan, bring your key in here, hurry!"

The girls scrambled into the next room where all that was visible of Jack was his back as he was leaning inside of a large wooden cupboard. Megan handed Jack the key. The door was hidden in a piece of the paneled back wall of the cupboard, similar to the wall that Megan had leaned on downstairs that had popped open to reveal the staircase. Jack had noticed that the back of the cupboard was not as deep as it should be, and on closer investigation, he noticed the small keyhole! Jack inserted the key into the keyhole, held his breath, and turned. The lock turned smoothly and the small door opened silently. Jack reached in and pulled out the contents of the secret hiding place. There were four wooden objects and a book.

"That's it? That's all that's in there?" asked Kendall.

"Let me see." She leaned into the opening and felt all around. There was nothing else inside. "I thought we'd find something really neat hidden inside. What are these things?" she asked disappointedly as she picked up one of the wooden tools.

"I know what these are," said Jack. "My father has some. These are wood planes. But why someone would hide them in here, well, beats me."

"What is this book?" asked Megan with a vague curiosity. She picked up the old and well used book and attempted to read from the cover, " 'Palladio Londinensis.' Oh, brother. I wish it was another diary or something," she said in a very dejected tone as she dropped the book back down to the floor.

Jack picked it up and thumbed through the pages. "Well, there are some really neat drawings in here. Cool house pictures, doors, stuff like that. I wonder how old this book is." He turned to the inside cover and read, "1734. This book was written in 1734! Do you realize how old this is?" he asked the girls.

They were not too impressed. Both of the cousins were feeling let down after finally finding Anah's secret hiding place, but not finding anything inside that belonged to Anah or was even of any interest.

"Well, I think this book and these planes are pretty cool. Let's take them back to your house and show them to your grandparents. Don't forget, we've found a lot of new clues that my mom can use to help us. And, we want to tell her about finding Joshua Walker, remember?"

"Oh, yeah. I almost forgot about that," said Megan with a sigh. "We should call your mom and ask her to come over. She wanted to see the sampler, too, so we can show her all of this stuff."

"Yeah, that's probably a good idea," said Kendall quietly. "I guess it's time to tell Grandma and Grandpa about the diary, too."

Chapter 13
Cousins

 The children gathered up the letters, the diary, the old family Bible, the wood planes and the old book and carried everything back to the Bayleys' house. The girls' mood had lightened by the time they got back to the house. They set everything on the dining room table and went upstairs to get the rest of their treasures that they had stored inside the old blanket chest. Meanwhile, Jack had telephoned his mother and Mrs. Walker was on her way over. Jack hadn't told her exactly what they had found, but just that they had found some new clues and needed her help.

"My goodness. Did you find all of this in that box you bought at the auction?" Mrs. Walker asked the girls.

"Well, most of it. It's kind of a long story. But we found out some information in one of the letters that we thought you would want to know about," said Kendall. "We found a person named Joshua Walker in one of the letters!"

"Joshua Walker?" Mrs. Walker looked over at Jack in surprise. "Jack, do you think that you found out something about your great, great, great grandfather?" she asked excitedly.

"I think so, Mom. Here's the letter! You should read

this and see what you think," he said as he handed his mother the final letter from Eliza.

"All I was able to learn about Joshua Walker is that he was born in 1795 and later married a young woman named Elizabeth."

Megan flashed a look at Kendall. "He was married to someone named Elizabeth? Are you sure? Could someone named Elizabeth have been called Eliza?" Megan asked Mrs. Walker excitedly.

"Oh, yes, Eliza is a nickname for Elizabeth. Wait, do you think that's the Eliza from your letters? Let me see this," she said as she started to read the letter.

Just then, the front door opened and in walked Grandma. "Well, it looks like we're having a party in here. What's all the excitement about?" she asked.

"The kids have just shown me this remarkable letter, Elizabeth. I think I may have found another clue to my family genealogy!"

"Well, speaking of genealogy and family trees," began Grandma, "I have just come from the library where I've been doing a little bit of investigating myself. You girls got me interested in finding out more about our family. When we drew our family tree, I only was able to go back as far as Grandpa's grandfather. So, I did some checking, and I was able to find out who his great grandfather was." She unfolded a piece of paper that had been stuck in her pocket. "His great grandfather was a man named Edwin Bayley, who was born in 1862."

The girls and Jack were stunned. They remembered reading the name Edwin Bayley in the old Bible they found in Anah's house just an hour before. "Grandma, you need to look at this," said Kendall.

"My, where did you find this old family Bible?" she

asked.

"It was in the cottage. We just found it. Grandma, this is a Bible from Anah's family, the Anah from the letters, and it has that same name in it, Edwin Bayley. Look," said Megan as she handed her grandmother the opened Bible page that showed the family tree.

A few minutes later, Grandpa arrived with a big announcement. "Good news, kids. I checked with the auctioneer and found out about our blanket chest. It turns out that the man who put it in the auction had it because his father bought it from my grandfather years and years ago, when he was cleaning out the little cottage. But luckily, no one bothered to open it up or do anything with the contents. So, now we have it back again. Looks like it belongs in this family after all."

With all of the revelations of the day, no one was too surprised at Grandpa's news. "What's going on here, anyway?" he asked as he looked around the room at Mrs. Walker, Jack, Grandma, Megan, and Kendall.

Everyone started talking excitedly at the same time. "Whoa, slow down! Let's start at the beginning. Megan, you go first. Now, I want to hear the whole story," Grandpa said.

Over an hour later, everyone in the room knew all about the false bottom in the blanket chest, the hidden key, the diary, about Anah's father and the blanket chest, the secret door in Anah's house and the contents of that hiding place. Mrs. Walker had brought along the large family tree she was working on with the children and she was writing notes the whole time. When the girls and Jack had finished with their wonderful story, she asked for everyone's attention.

"This is the most fun I've had in a long time, I must say. But has anyone realized what other keys you kids have discovered?" she asked.

Everyone shook their heads, not sure what Mrs. Walker meant.

"The family tree holds the key to the real story," she said with a wide smile as she held it up for them all to see. "It tells me that Megan and Kendall, cousins, are distant relatives of Anah and Eliza, who were also cousins."

The girls beamed!

"And," Mrs. Walker continued, "It also tells me that Jack here is a distant relative of Eliza Watson and Joshua Walker, making him a distant cousin of you girls. Congratulations! You're all cousins. Our family just got bigger," she announced with a smile.

The three children looked at each other in disbelief, then everyone was laughing and talking at the same time.

A few weeks later, they were all sitting in the Bayleys' living room again, with three additional guests joining them: Megan's mother and father, and Mr. Parks from the museum. A more confident Megan was the center of attention, filling her parents in on some of the details of their discoveries while the others listened closely. Kendall had just finished chatting on the telephone with her mother and was happy. Both of her parents were arriving the next day for a short vacation with Kendall.

Grandpa cleared his throat, looked around the room

slowly with a growing smile, and began to read from the Eastern Shore News:

Local Children Uncover Secrets from the Past:

Megan Brown and Kendall Scott, granddaughters of Warren and Elizabeth Bayley of Accomac, made a series of unique discoveries this summer while vacationing on the Eastern Shore. The cousins purchased a box at a local auction that held many valuable antiques from the early 1800s. Among their treasures were a sampler, a silver spoon given by Agnes Kerr in 1809, and several wonderfully preserved letters written in 1809 and 1810.

The girls also discovered a diary that had been hidden away for nearly 200 years. The diary contained valuable information identifying an important early joiner, or carpenter, a man named Edwin Matthews.

In addition to learning the name of that joiner, the girls, along with their cousin, Jack Walker, of Accomac, unearthed a collection of antique wooden molding planes believed to have once belonged to Edwin Matthews.

Along with the planes, the children discovered a first edition of the extremely rare architectural resource, "Palladio Londinensis; or, The London Art of Building," which was published in 1734. The book is one of only seven first edition copies known in existence in the world. It was found in a secret compartment in an abandoned cottage on the Bayleys' property.

Further research into the discoveries made by these children has led to the identity of two early decoy carvers: Daniel Edmonds and Joshua Walker, both now known to be distant relatives of Jack Walker.

This very important collection of early local artifacts is on loan to the Eastern Shore of Virginia Historical Society and will be on display at Kerr Place in Onancock, for the remainder of this year. After that, the collection will join other significant artifacts as part of a large, early American history exhibit that will be touring the United States for two years.

Brown, Scott, and Walker are collaborating on a children's book about their adventures. They are being assisted by Miss Brown's mother, well known mystery writer, Rachel Brown, daughter of the Bayleys.

The End

Author's Note

Although the characters and the story are fictional, the places named in **The Hidden Key** are real. The towns mentioned are located on the Virginia Eastern Shore, a 70-mile long stretch of Virginia that separates the Atlantic Ocean and the Chesapeake Bay. Settlers began living in Accomac, Virginia in the 1600s, and Kerr Place was the home that John and Agnes Ker built in 1799 in Onancock, Virginia. Kerr Place is now a museum and the home of the Eastern Shore of Virginia Historical Society. Onancock, a waterfront town on the Onancock Creek, was chartered in 1680.

The joiners named in the story are fictional, however, the Eastern Shore raised-panel furniture is an authentic style that was made by the local house carpenters of the time between 1730 and 1830. Examples of this furniture are in private collections of families both on and off the Shore.

GLOSSARY

butter paddle
> A wooden paddle used to press the water out of freshly churned butter and used to press butter into molds.

carding
> Combing or brushing fibers like wool, cotton, and flax to get them ready to spin.

cat's cradle
> A child's game played with a string looped over the fingers to form designs.

curator
> The person in charge of a museum and its collections.

Eastern Shore
> A 70-mile long peninsula of Virginia between the Atlantic Ocean and the Chesapeake Bay.

family tree
> Generations of one family, ancestors (those who came before, like parents, grandparents) and descendants (offspring or children), shown on a branching chart like a tree that indicates relationships (parents, grandparents, children, grandchildren).

firedogs
> Metal supports that hold logs in a fireplace. Sometimes called andirons.

genealogy
> The study of the history of a family.

hallmark
> The mark stamped on gold and silver articles that indicate the maker, when, and where it was made.

homespun
> Cloth made of yarn that was spun at home using a spinning wheel.

hornbook
> A sheet of parchment with the alphabet on it, mounted on a board and protected by a thin, clear layer of horn.

Jamestown
> A colonial settlement that started in 1607 at the mouth of the James River in Virginia.

joiner
> A carpenter that does woodwork inside a house like the doors, stairs, and molding.

niddy noddy
> A wooden stretcher that is used to wind handspun yarn onto to keep it straight.

penknife
> A small pocketknife originally used in making quill pens.

press
> A cupboard used to store clothes, linens, or books.

quill
> A bird feather cut to use as a pen.

sampler, sampleth
> A piece of cloth embroidered with the alphabet and designs used to display needlework skills.

spinning
> Making yarn or thread by twisting the fibers together, usually with a spinning wheel.

spooling
> Winding spun yarn or thread onto a spool.

sugar cutters
> Metal scissor-like cutters used to cut chunks of sugar from a sugar loaf.

ACTIVITIES

MAKE A YARN DOLL

*You can make a yarn doll just like
Megan and Kendall made in the story.*

You will need:
> Yarn in any color
> Cardboard
> Scissors
> Small ball for head: rubber,
> ping pong, or foam
> Glue

Directions:
1. Cut the cardboard the height you want your doll. For an 8" doll, make the cardboard 8" high by about 5" wide. For a taller doll, make the cardboard taller. Wrap the yarn around the cardboard the long way about 20 times.

2. Cut a short piece of yarn and tie it tightly around the wrapped yarn at the top of the cardboard to hold all the yarn together in a bunch. This will be the top of the head.

3. Cut through each piece of the wrapped yarn at the bottom of the cardboard (at the feet).

4. Put the small ball for the head underneath the yarn where it is tied, and cover it completely with yarn. Use a short piece of yarn to tie around the yarn under the ball, to form the neck.

5. Divide the yarn that hangs down from the head into four parts. Two will be arms and two will be legs.

6. Tie a short piece of yarn about halfway down each arm to hold the strands of yarn together. Trim off to make the arms shorter than the legs.

7. Tie a piece of yarn around the body of the doll to form the waist.

8. Tie short pieces of yarn around the bottom of each leg to hold the yarn strands together.

9. Decorate with buttons, ribbons, fabric scraps, or other colors of yarn to finish your doll. Use glue to attach eyes, mouth, and hair. Now your yarn doll is ready!

MAKE A SAND CANDLE

You will need:
> Cardboard box
> Sand
> Water
> Spoon
> Empty can with label removed
> Paraffin wax
> Saucepan
> Stove
> Small metal weight (nut or washer)
> Hot mitt
> Waxed string for wick
> Optional: crayon shavings for color

Warning: *This activity requires a stove and hot wax, so only do this activity with an adult assisting.*

Directions:
1. Fill the box about 3/4 full of damp sand. Pack it down tightly and smooth the top surface.

2. Using a spoon and your hands, make a hole in the sand the shape you want for your candle. Make it fairly deep, but don't dig all the way to the bottom of the box.

3. Have an adult melt the paraffin wax on the stove in a dry can that is placed inside a saucepan of water (forming a double boiler). Slowly heat the wax until it melts. Add crayon shavings to the melted wax to add color if you want.

4. Using a hot mitt, have the adult slowly pour the melted wax into the hole in the sand. This will make your candle. Get your wick ready by attaching the weight to the end of the string. Wait until the wax has cooled enough to form a skin on the top surface, then lower your wick, weighted end first, down into the hot wax. Be careful not to touch the wax with your fingers as it will burn you.

5. Leave the candle to cool over night. The next day, dig your candle out of the sand. Brush off the sand and you have a finished candle. Let an adult light the candle for you on the next special occasion.

Print with a Block of Soap

You will need:

    Bar of soap, any kind
    Pencil or pen
    Small sponge
    Tempera paint or water-based printing ink
    Small bowl or plate
    Masking tape
    Vegetable peeler
    Paper

Directions:

1. Plan a simple design and draw the design onto the bar of soap with a pencil or pen.

2. Wrap masking tape around the sharp middle section of the vegetable peeler. Have an adult help you with this. Use the peeler to cut around your design leaving the design raised up and the background cut away.

3. Be sure to always use your carving tool pushing it away from you to avoid getting cut.

4. When your design is cut away neatly, put the paint or ink onto a small plate or in a bowl. Then dip your sponge into the paint and gently pat the sponge onto your design.

5. Turn the bar of soap over so that the painted side is down and press onto a clean sheet of paper. Or, you may want to set the soap down with the paint side up and lay

the paper over the top of the soap. Gently rub the paper again the soap then lift up. Your design will be printed on the paper.

HOMEMADE BERRY INK

This ink is fun to make at home. When it is finished, drip your quill pen or art pen into the ink and you are ready to write just like the early colonists did.

You will need:
    1 cup of berries: blackberries, strawberries, raspberries, blueberries.
    1 teaspoon of vinegar
    1 teaspoon of salt
    Small jar with lid (baby food jars are great for this!)
    Small strainer and spoon
    Food coloring

Directions:
1. Remove the lid from the jar and set aside. Hold the strainer over the top of the jar.

2. Put a few berries at a time into the strainer and crush them with the back of the spoon so that the juice runs into the jar. You can use one type of berry or mix several kinds together.

3. When you have finished making berry juice, add the vinegar and salt into the jar and stir until it dissolves. If you wish, you can add a few drops of food coloring to make the ink darker.

4. Make just a small amount of berry ink at a time as it spoils quickly. Keep the lid on the jar when you are finished with the ink and store in the refrigerator to extend the life of your ink.

PRACTICE YOUR HANDWRITING

Early colonists took great care and pride in their penmanship. You can practice writing in this old fashioned style by copying the following alphabet. For best results, use a calligraphy pen, which will give you writing that looks the most like letters written with a quill pen. You can use this special style of writing for addressing envelopes, writing letters, and making gift cards. If you have a favorite poem or saying, writing it using pretty lettering makes a special keepsake and a thoughtful gift. Mount the poem onto colored paper or put it into a frame to keep it safe.

My Name:_____

A Favorite Saying:_____

_____

_____

A B C D E F G
H I J K L M
N O P Q R S T
U V W X Y Z

abcdefghijklm
nopqrstuvwxyz
1234567890

MAKE YOUR OWN FAMILY TREE

You can trace the genealogy of your own family by asking your parents, grandparents, and other relatives for information. You can decide what type of information you need. You can use just names, or you can add in birthdates, town or city where they were born, date of marriages, and dates when people died. Try to find out full names (first, middle, last) as you may see that some names have been given to several people in your family. After you have collected your data below, fill it in on the chart on the following pages. This will begin your family tree.

MY FAMILY INFORMATION

My name, birthdate, place of birth:

My brother's/sister's name, birthdate, place of birth:

My brother's/sister's name, birthdate, place of birth:

My brother's/sister's name, birthdate, place of birth:

My brother's/sister's name, birthdate, place of birth:

FATHER'S FAMILY:

My father's name, birthdate, place of birth, date of marriage:

> My grandfather's (father's father) name, birthdate, place of birth, date of marriage:

>> Grandfather's parents (my great grandparents!)
>> His mother:

>> His father:
> My grandmother's (father's mother) name, birthdate, place of birth:

Grandmother's parents (my great grandparents!)
Her mother:

Her father:

MOTHER'S FAMILY:

My mother's name, birthdate, place of birth:

My grandfather's (mother's father) name, birthdate, place of birth, date of marriage:

Grandfather's parents (my great grandparents!)
His mother:

His father:

My grandmother's (mother's mother) name, birthdate, place of birth:

Grandmother's parents (my great grandparents!)
Her mother:

Her father:

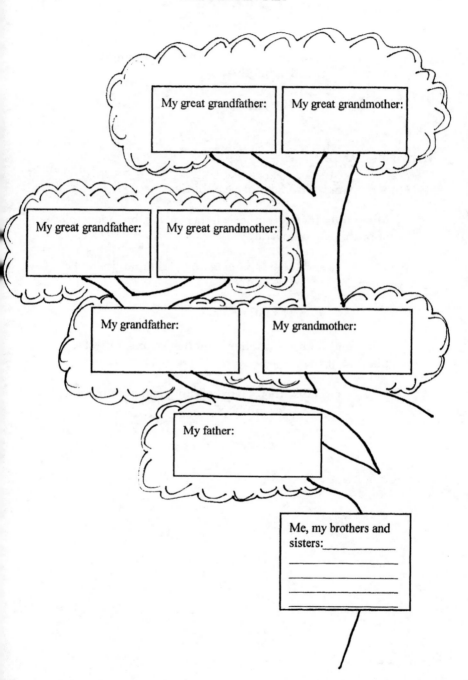

My great grandfather:

My great grandmother:

My great grandfather:

My great grandmother:

My grandfather:

My grandmother:

My father:

Me, my brothers and
sisters:_____
_____
_____
_____

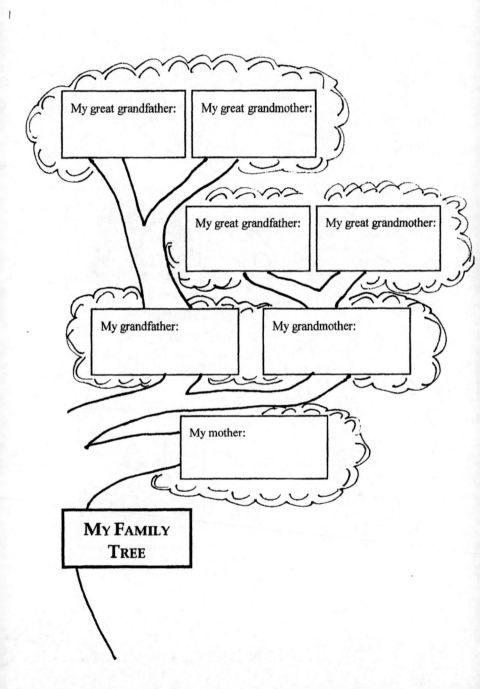

My great grandfather:

My great grandmother:

My great grandfather:

My great grandmother:

My grandfather:

My grandmother:

My mother:

MY FAMILY TREE

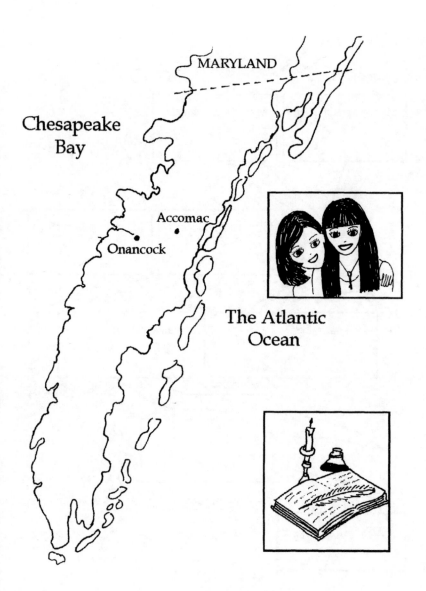

MAP OF THE EASTERN SHORE OF VIRGINIA

Notes for Teachers

It is important for children to study history in order to better understand their society and be well equiped to face the future. When children are aware of how people in other times lived, they gain a new perspective of their own lives.

The Hidden Key can be a useful resource for elementary school teachers. In addition to being an enjoyable book for a teacher to read chapter by chapter to a class or for student silent reading, it also helps teachers meet the Standards of Learning for Virginia Public Schools in both the English and History subject areas.

In English, students at a variety of grade levels are able to use **The Hidden Key** to meet Reading/Literature, Writing, and Research goals. You will note that this book has a glossary at the end which can serve as a starting point for further research for interested students. The activities included at the end can be done either at home or at school, and the genealogy portion under "Family Tree" can serve as an interesting activity that can involve parents along with their children.

Using Fry's Readability Graph, **The Hidden Key** is written at approximately a fifth grade level, with an interest level of ages 8 - 12.

In meeting the History SOL's (Standards of Learning), the following is a partial list of goals by grade level that apply to this publication:

GRADE ONE - **History 1.1**   *Comparing everyday life in different times. The children in the story have virtues that teach good character.*

GRADE TWO - **History 2.2**   *Compare how local rural communities have changed over time.*

History 2.3   *Introduce the Indian settlements on the Eastern Shore.*

GRADE THREE - **History 3.3**   *Introduce early settlements in the Virginia colony.*

GRADE FOUR - **History 4.7**   *Historical analysis skills using primary sources: artifacts, diaries, letters, and documents using fictionalized characters.*

GRADE FIVE - **History 5.6**   *Growth and change in America 1801-1861.*

History 5.9   *Develop skills for historical analysis using fictionalized primary sources.*

NOTES

NOTES

SHEEPDOG PRESS

"Woof!"